Trouble the Water

By Melvin Dixon

Winner of the 1989
Nilon Award

University of Colorado
and
Fiction Collective Two
Boulder • Normal • Brooklyn

This book is the winner of the 1989 Charles H. and N. Mildred Nilon
Excellence in Minority Fiction Award, sponsored by the University of
Colorado and Fiction Collective Two.

Published jointly by the University of Colorado at Boulder, and Fiction
Collective Two, with assistance from the National Endowment for the Arts;
the support of the Publications Center, University of Colorado at Boulder;
and the cooperation of Brooklyn College, Illinois State University, Normal,
and Teachers & Writers Collaborative.

Forward all inquiries to: Fiction Collective Two, English Department
Publications Center, Campus Box 494, University of Colorado at Boulder,
Boulder, CO 80309-0494.

The characters in this novel arise from the author's imagination; any
resemblance to actual persons is purely coincidental.

Library of Congress Cataloging in Publication
Dixon, Melvin.
    Trouble the Water
I. Title.

ISBN: 0-932511-23-6
ISBN: 0-932511-24-4 (pbk.)

Printed by Edwards Brothers Inc.
Manufactured in the United States of America.

for my father

When there is no history
there is no metaphor;
a blind nation in storm
mauls its own harbors.
                    —Michael S. Harper,
                        Song: I Want a Witness

Wade in the water
Wade in the water, children,
Wade in the water
God's gonna trouble the water.
                    —Traditional

Jordan was six and riding the pine fence that surrounded the cornfield. He squeezed the rough crossboards between his legs and took off on a wild, fast gallop. He held himself high over the river of green leaves and yellow-brown silk. Clinging to the waves of grass between the field and the woods were junebugs round and shiny like iridescent dimes but easier to hold on to. Jordan sat perched between the woods full of the boogey men his grandmother conjured up at will and Mother Harriet herself working the clothesline a few yards away. "Look at me, Gran'Mama," he yelled, waving both arms and almost losing balance, "Look at me!"

"Boy, you watch yourself," she called through the clothespins in her mouth. Jordan barely heard the raspy voice, but he searched the woods behind him just the same. Then he tried walking the fence like a tightrope. Poised in balance, he was taller than Mother Harriet and out of reach of the corn. He sucked in his breath and inched forward one foot at a time. When he tried to turn around he missed a step and met the green leaves slapping his face and legs. From below Jordan saw for the first time the rotting cracked notch at the end of the fence. The corn brushed back into place.

"Didn't I tell you?" said Mother Harriet, poking her wrinkled face through the clothes and laughing. "Boy, you's a mess," she chuckled and went back to her work.

Jordan broke free the dangling, broken crossboard and wielded it like a sword. The dense cornfield was now a jungle filled with vegetal monsters and giants and elephants

1

and dinosaurs, dragonflies and junebugs, too, catching sun in the prisms of their wings and bodies. Jordan slashed and chopped and maimed and stabbed the weeds between the rows, then gathered the sparkling insects as his prize. Perched high on the broken fence again, he surveyed the imaginary carnage as the junebugs made lines of crawling gems along his arms.

Mother Harriet kept an eye on Jordan as she worked. The sun glittered from the Vaseline in his hair and the sweat dotting his brow. "Such a pretty boy," Harriet said to herself. "Just like his Mama." She pulled his underwear and socks from the coils of wash and hung them in place. When she bent into the basket again for her shirts and kerchiefs, she saw the head of a shadow. Then more of it crept under her from behind. She turned around quickly, dropping a wet blouse in the dirt. She saw that it was a man. She studied his mustache, his overalls spotted red and smelling of urine and fifty-cent wine. In his fat, callused hands he held a package the size of a shoebox wrapped in yellowing newspaper that he shifted from arm to arm. When she saw the scar that made his lips curl down, she knew him, Jake Williams, without the mustache or the dirty clothes.

"Hi're you, Miss Henry," he said from the side of his mouth as if the scar were fresh.

Mother Harriet said nothing. Her chest sank, her skin pulled tight. Jake tried to smile, and that made her stomach heave. She bit her lips and set her back straight. When she noticed Jordan watching them so keenly from the fence, she got more angry than afraid.

"Just come by to see how you doing, Miss Henry," said Jake, shifting the newspaper surprise again.

"Ain't nothing for you here," said Harriet. Her voice

2

edged up from her belly. From the pine fence, Jordan watched them and listened.

"Ain't nothing for you here," she said. "Chloe's dead."

"I knows that, Miss Henry. I reckon I ought to know. She was my girl. Everybody here to Rockingham know that."

"Humph."

"She was my pretty pecan."

"You's nothing, Jake. And ain't never been more'n nothing for Chloe."

"How you know, Miss Henry? You talk to the dead?"

Harriet said nothing. Jordan followed the blur of newsprint on the shifting, nervous package.

"She was my girl, Chloe was. We was in love."

"Don't mess with me this morning, Jake."

He set the newspaper package on the ground between them.

Mother Harriet stepped away from the package and wrung out the last piece of laundry. She fixed it with a pin. "Ain't nothing for you here, Jake. Nothing."

Jordan stood up on the fence to get a better view. He held on with hands and feet.

"Folks say I got a boy."

Mother Harriet stopped working.

"They tells me—" he started.

"You stay away from that boy, you hear me. He's nothing to you." The anger cramping Harriet's stomach began to boil and brought a sour taste to her mouth. Her belly was a bubbling washpot, forging knives.

"A right good-looking fella at that," said Jake, turning to Jordan. He picked up the newspaper package. "I brought him a present. Something he's gonna like." He started for the cornfield.

3

"You stop right there, Jake. You keep away from that boy."

Jake walked to the field.

Mother Harriet ran into the house and got Pa Henry's shotgun from beside the bed.

"You keep away from that boy!"

Jordan stared from the fence, his eyes wide as targets.

Jake kept moving.

"I got me a shotgun and ain't 'fraid to use it. Not on no sorry nigger like you."

Jake was close enough to Jordan's face to recognize his own nose and eyes. The lips were different. No scars. The boy was silent. Jake turned back to Mother Harriet and met the shotgun raised to her squinting face, her knuckles hugging the trigger. Jake stepped forward. One shot split the air. Then another.

"I ain't afraid," she said.

No one moved, no one spoke. The trigger clicked again. Jake dropped his shoulders. He turned away from Jordan and the broken fence. "Why you got to be like that, Miss Henry?" He lowered his head and tucked the newspaper surprise back under his arm. He walked out of the corn-field, past the clothesline and stopped at the red dirt driveway.

"I'll be back one day, Miss Henry. You can count on that. And you won't be nowhere around. You been living off the dead long enough." Through his slanted lips Jake started to laugh. "Shit, woman, you won't be nowhere around."

Jake left the yard. Mother Harriet kept her bony hand at the trigger. Jordan felt his arms for the glittering junebugs, but they had gone.

4

ONE
Trouble About My Grave

1

Drunk with thaw from the Carr Mountains, the Pee Dee River raised its muddy arms and hugged the shore. Months into spring the river was still drinking. Ripples on its surface arched into blue-black lips that puckered and belched with every swallow. As the river swelled, hilltops along the Blue Ridge Mountains seemed to shrink. A low, thick fog inching out of the North Carolina morning hung a veil of heat over all and narrowed the horizon. Under a silver green sky the water glistened like a bolt of wrinkled satin. But when it rose, the river became as sloppy and inebriated as molasses.

At night the black surface of the water was pure snake-skin. Ripples burst on its surface without a sound. Flies and mosquitoes knitted their buzz and whine into the cooling air. Crickets sang soprano, bullfrogs bass. And the face of the water opened its many mouths to catch the kisses of car headlights sweeping across the Hardison Bridge. At the rattle of pickup trucks riding the heels of twilight, those mouths became ears filling up with sound.

Wide and long the Pee Dee started way up in the Blue Ridge as the Yadkin River. It flowed south and east until it joined the Uharie in the Piedmont and gave its name and granite color to the village near Lilesville, midway between Wadesboro and Rockingham. It would reach farther down into South Carolina, gather red clay and yellow silt as the Little Pee Dee, ease into the Winyah Bay at Georgetown, then break water at the Atlantic.

One afternoon Mitch followed his brother Beauford to the water. He knew all about the Pee Dee from what Harriet Henry and Addie Miller said about the Confederate gold hidden somewhere between the bridge and Blewett Falls, and from his mother Maggie telling how Rev. Franklin led the church membership class there for baptism. Each day Mitch rode the schoolbus across the riverbridge, but he just didn't see the water for all his looking at the short hills rolling back from the whitewashed plank houses and yards full of wood chips. He played tag with Ruthie and fought with Beauford over whose turn it was to stack kindling for cookfires or draw water from the pump for the chilly morning face wash. When he did notice the river glittering in the warm spring sun, he wanted a closer look and feel, not Maggie's church songs about deep rivers or Harriet moaning about camp ground.

Mitch was only eight, too small to go to the water alone. He waited until he had traded fifteen of his best baseball cards and five squares of chewing gum to Beauford, three years older, just to take him. Together they slipped off the schoolbus with their friends who lived closer to the Pee Dee than their stop two roads yonder by Addie Miller's shack store. The boys left their sister Ruthie on the creaking, mustard-colored bus with the letters Anson County Public Schools peeling from its sides. Ruthie promised not to tell. From the side window, she waved to them as Beauford and Mitch mixed in among the children going their usual way home. The bus lurched forward, leaving them in a spray of red dust, ricocheting gravel, sputtering exhaust fumes.

Mitch sucked in his breath. He was alone with Beauford, the highway, and the river rushing downstream in a noisy traffic of its own.

"We here now," said Beauford. "You got any more Dodgers?"

"You wanted Yankees before."

"So I changed my mind."

Mitch pretended to look for the extra cards in his lunchbox. It was empty. "Ain't got no more, Beau."

"You got some back home, don't you?"

"Naw," said Mitch.

"Bet you can find some."

Mitch turned away from Beauford and scanned the asphalt road. The river lay shimmering on the other side. His heart jumped. His face grew hot and flushed. He was this close to adventure and now Beauford had to start acting up, being bossy, lowering his voice to sound like their father Jeremiah about to set a switch to Mitch's behind.

"You wanted to come so bad. We here now."

"Yep, we here now," said Mitch.

They would not stay long. After an hour or two along the remaining sliver of riverbank they would walk back home before Jeremiah left work at the peach processing plant. Ruthie would cover for them, since they were supposed to be cleaning up Harriet's yard while Ruthie fixed the old woman a plate of dinner. For the boys, the afternoon was just right for exploring the riverbank, the water, maybe even find a turtle, a frog, or anything alive.

Beauford crossed the highway first. Behind him rushed a short stream of cars. Then came a truck that sent tremors lumbering through the hollow curve of road above the bridge.

"Come on," said Beauford. "Don't be no sissy now."

"I ain't no sissy," called Mitch above the din of traffic.

"You is," said Beauford, turning his back.

"Wait up, Beau!"

"We ain't got all day."

Mitch didn't move. His aluminum lunchbox clanged at his legs. When the cars had passed he heard the running, coursing river. Beauford was about to descend the dirt path

9

leading to the fishermen's parking lot without him. The river gurgled and splashed with its clumsy arms and lips and wide, broad shoulders. Beauford moved farther ahead. "Wait up," said Mitch, but he wasn't the only one the river had called.

Mitch tripped over his own lunchbox. His face hit the dirt and asphalt. Luckily there were no cars. He dusted himself off, looked both ways, and darted across the road. Just as suddenly a truck rounded a corner, zoomed by. The wake of wind brought a bone-tingling chill. Mitch's lunchbox caught a glimmer of sun, clanged empty and cold against him. He shuddered. Ahead of him was Beauford moving through the sand lot and skipping stones over the water with a speed and power Mitch thought he needed. Whizz. Pop! Beauford had reached the riverbank and the swirling, mud-streaked water.

The closer Mitch came the larger grew his eyes. He couldn't get enough of the ever-expansive Pee Dee. His nose twitched with the acrid smell of highwater and soggy loam. His sneakers squeaked from water oozing between canvas and rubber. Mitch didn't worry. He was just glad to be there. "Golly," he said, taking it all in.

"That all you got to say?" asked Beauford, reaching for more stones.

"Yeah. Golly." Mitch watched as the water inched to his toes. "It's bigger than I thought."

"Must be a mile wide," added Beauford in a mix of caution and awe. Then, suddenly, his tone sharpened, "Ain't no mile."

"How you know so much?"

"Cause I just know."

"We better not go too far, huh, Beau?"

"You a fraidy cat, Mitch?"

"Naw."

10

"Me neither."

They didn't move from the spot.

Mitch remembered Rev. Franklin's preaching after a baptism late one Sunday. The deacons and elders were all dressed in white. They had just come from the Pee Dee. Some had towels draped around their shivering shoulders. One man started to sing and other voices joined in, repeating the rush and run of the water. The song and the rhythm terrified Mitch. Rev. Franklin hawked his sermon. And Mother Harriet added her trembling alto to the chorus. She sang, "w-w-w-wade in the w-w-w-water," her words tremoring like waves. Jeremiah patted him and Beauford on the head, smiled, and said to Harriet, "My boys is next." Harriet whispered to them, "God bless you, chi'ren." Mitch got even more afraid. Singing or praying or just saying howdy-do, Mother Harriet's voice always made Mitch squirm. And he wondered what he'd feel when the preacher would duck him under and lift him up, his cheeks puffed out, shoulders hunched in against the cold. But what if the preacher held him down too long, or forgot to lift him out?

A truck speeding across the riverbridge behind him broke the spell. Beauford sent another flat stone whistling over the water. It skipped three times, then sank like a gumdrop into a hungry mouth. The Pee Dee belched, spraying insects with its foamy saliva.

"Hear that, Mitch? I can make them whistle." Beauford sent another stone in a low cross throw to the right. Skip, skip, skip, plop! The hungry water ate.

"Let me try," said Mitch. He set his lunchbox down and raised his arms high, too high. No skip. Plop.

"You got to have a flat stone, Mitch, and flick your wrist just as you let go. Don't you know anything?"

Skip. Skip. A whistle of granite and mud. A low swallow.

11

Ripples circling out. A shimmering bull's-eye.

"Later for you, Beauford. I'm gonna find me some turtles." Mitch walked away as his sneakers started to squish. Sand gritted and scratched them; he took them off and laid them on a boulder to dry.

"I'm-a tell Mama," said Beauford. "Getting your feet wet."

"They be dry soon. Don't *you* know anything?"

"I know Mama gonna be upside your head."

The touch of riverwater on his feet made Mitch want to wade further in and he did. The Pee Dee roused itself out of a drunken stupor and the satisfying gulps of Beauford's whistling stones. It stretched its slippery, frothy hands to reach the younger boy, soften the ground beneath him, tickle his ankles. Goose bumps crawled up Mitch's legs. Soon, he was warm. The lapping water welcomed him. Mitch grabbed his empty lunchbox and waded further in. Beauford, oblivious to the easy meeting of river and boy, slapped at the foaming shoreline with a stick. He'd go no farther than that. Why slip and get all wet when he didn't even know how to swim? The thought of bottomless water paralyzed him. Beauford stayed close to the shore. He cut another switch and scratched his name into the sand.

Mitch was in up to his calves. He followed the contour of the shore to a section of woods where the river thickened to liquid mud and smelled like gun metal. Ahead of him appeared a gravelbar with clumps of grass braving earth and water.

"Look at me, Beau," Mitch called to the shore.

Beauford dropped the switch. He picked up a rock.

"You bet' not hit me."

"Will if I want to."

"You bet' not," said Mitch, shielding himself with the empty lunchbox. He moved farther along the shore, leaving Beauford and his rocks behind.

Suddenly, from the shallow water came slimy things touching him, and when he bent for a closer look, Mitch saw more of them swimming around him. He cupped his hands, scooped up three, then another and another until he had six tadpoles in his lunchbox. He waded back to Beauford, who was sitting on a log and whacking the water with another switch.

"I couldn't find me no turtles, Beau," he said, watching gnats circle Beauford's head. Beauford swung with the stick.

"Look out, Beau. You almost hit me."

Beauford swung at the gnats again. Mitch got out of the way.

"I told you so."

"Naw, you didn't."

"Them turtles and frogs ain't come out yet. It's too early. It still gets cold out. You got to wait until it warms up some."

"Oh yeah?"

"Don't you know anything, Mitch?"

"I got me some tadpoles, though."

"You call them things tadpoles? You ought to put them back and let them grow some. You can come back in the summer and get them when they're frogs and growed up."

Mitch held up his lunchbox. Water dripped through the aluminum seams.

"You can't even keep them cause they need this kind of water to live in and eat in. Don't you know anything?"

Mitch fished through his lunchbox, then emptied it back into the river. The bigger tadpoles plopped back like pebbles. They didn't skip across the water's surface. Mitch don't have that sleight of hand. He walked back to the shore, the lunchbox slamming empty against his legs.

"Maybe we can find a snake or something, huh, Beau?"

"Aw, Mitch, let's go home."

"Just look around some. It won't take long."

The boys moved into the wooded area behind the shoreline. The grass they waded through moved like waves of brushed hair. The earth was firm. The boys overturned logs and flat stones in their search. Under a rain-swollen log, soft as cork, was a shiny bulge that slithered deeper into the soil.

"Golly, Beauford. A snake."

"Ain't it gonna bite?"

"Naw."

Its young climbed wildly after the retreating hump. Mitch pulled one up into his hands where it curled and uncurled, darting its pointed head from the coils. The tongue tapped nervously at Mitch's palm.

"You got 'em, Mitch. You gonna keep it?"

"Sure, if Mama lets me."

"Can I hold it a little?"

"Be careful, now. It's still a baby."

"How you know it ain't a coach-whip or a moccasin? They kill you."

"I just know."

Mitch and Beauford passed the baby snake between them like a stretched rubber band. The sun lowered behind the hills and told them it was time to head home. The river reflected the streaks of sunset, and Mitch, feeling the cool air, rubbed his legs together to shed the itchy patches of sand. Birds cawed in the dimming sky and flew back to the hills.

"I'm getting hungry," said Beauford. "Let's go home."

14

"You always hungry."

The boys made their way back to the riverbank, then Beauford stopped short. They were heading the wrong way. He turned around and Mitch followed him, but the river-bridge was nowhere in sight. The humming cars were gone. Mitch caught his breath. What he suddenly feared was true. They had been circling the river all this time without know-ing it.

The woods thickened on both sides of the water. Ever-greens and brush rose up everywhere. The boys stood together; neither spoke. A hush fell over the woods and the water. Pine needles cushioned Mitch's feet, half covered with sand as if one foot preferred water, the other land.

"See what you did, Mitch. You got us lost."

"How I get us lost?"

"Worrying over them tadpoles and snakes."

"You didn't have to follow me. You could-a said something."

"And have Pappa whup me for losing you? Naw."

Mitch moved back into the pine needles, beyond a thick line of brush. The sweet and pungent smell of bark and evergreen filled everywhere, but the silence was frightening.

Night was coming on.

Beauford spotted the trail first, then called to Mitch. It was nothing more than a clearing in front of briars and tree moss, but the tongue of trail had been pounded hard by many feet, as if boys their age had also visited the Pee Dee decades earlier and left their mark. Above it lay an eroded stretch of gravel and clay. Beauford pointed madly, "There, there, see it, Mitch?"

"What?"

"Addie Miller's chimney. Smoke coming out."

"Naw, you lying. I can't see nothing."

"Look!"

And sure enough, there was smoke, a chimney, and a lip of asphalt. The path was a shortcut through the pines. They wouldn't get any more lost trying to find their way back to Highway 74. Ahead was Route 145, heading past Addie Miller's shack store and on into Morven. It seemed so close. After ten minutes, the boys were still tramping through the bush, the pines and unseen gullies that lay between the clearing, the river, and the road home. The whisk of shrubs against their clothes drowned out the fading sound of the Pee Dee, nestling back into its alcoholic slumber.

Beauford walked right into a circle of ashes and bits of charred wood. Mitch found a rusty can of beans or soup, he couldn't tell which. Beside it lay a broken green tinted bottle. These weren't boys passing through, but men. Hunters after possum, raccoon, squirrel. The setting sun made the objects luminous and sinister. Thank God for the familiar road. Mitch held his snake gingerly. His empty lunchbox clanged against his legs as it caught the last rays of sun.

"You think you so big, now, huh Mitch. But you was scared back there."

"Naw, I wasn't."

"You was."

"Shoot, next time I'm gonna swim and fish," said Mitch. "You wait."

"You be so scared, you drown, boy."

"Don't you sound all grown-up now, Beau. I led us out the woods."

"I showed you the path."

"You was scared."

"You was."

"You wait till Pappa teach me hunting, I'll show you about woods."

"I bet you shoot your feet off, Beau."

16

"Bet I won't."

"Look here," Mitch said, picking up a stone. He skipped it three times on the asphalt. The snake coiled and uncoiled about Mitch's other hand.

"That ain't nothing. Nothing at all."

The retreating sun cooled the road.

Suddenly, Mitch stopped short. "Golly, I forgot my shoes."

Beauford laughed. He hooted, "Well, I ain't going back with you to get them, that's for sure. We late already."

"What's Mama gonna say?"

"Nothing, just whup your behind." And Beauford laughed like he hadn't laughed in weeks, pointing at Mitch and holding in his sides.

"Golly," said Mitch. "What I'm gonna do now?"

Mother Harriet saw them. Even with Addie Miller sitting beside her on the creaking porch swing, she saw them. Her boy Jordan and his friend Mason Johnston from the next house over. This time she was sure it wasn't just in her clouded memory or time playing tricks with her eighty-some-odd years. There was Jordan a bit shorter than Mason as they crossed Route 145 near Addie's shack store, just below her part of the hill. They were turning now, past her dirt road, past the Johnston place, past Jeremiah Willis's fields, and soon they'd be climbing up to her. She saw them, and she heard them laughing, swatting mosquitoes, climbing up through the last rays of sunlight glittering from the fishing box in Jordan's hand. The gleaming metal held her attention. Jordan would be home in time to eat supper. She grinned and settled back in the porch swing to wait. Still, she'd better tell him to hurry on, don't be running his mouth with Mason while her greens were almost done and the cornbread just right for dunking in buttermilk. Don't tarry, boy, she almost said.

17

Addie Miller's feet tapped on the porch floor and kept tapping as Harriet's breathing increased, eyes grew wide, then squinted to see clearer. They were still there, so they must be real. Jordan and Mason coming home. Jordan, who stained the floor when he was born and sent Chloe, her only child, into frenzy and into silence. Chloe, who wore sunshine for a dress, who made love in the fields and broke her water at night. The tapping on the porch floor matched her own pacing then before the final pain, before she pulled the baby up from the bloodied sheets and floorboards. Addie Miller held a clean towel. Together they washed him, gave him breath, called him Jordan for the river Chloe had crossed.

Today the sun forgot Chloe and sent its last rays reflecting from the metal in the boy's small hand. Mother Harriet believed in what she saw. She eased herself up from the porch swing and leaned over the railing. "Jordan, you come home now. You come home. *Jordanyoucomehomenow.*" Although he was too far to hear, Harriet grinned at Addie Miller anyway and held her chest high.

"Lord, you's something else, Harriet," said Addie, and continued tapping her feet.

"You hear that?" asked Mitch.
"What?"
"That voice, that noise. Something."
"You sure?"
"Sure I'm sure."
"You trying to scare me, Mitch?"
"Look who's a sissy now."
"That wasn't no voice."
"Was so."
"You lying, Mitch. You better be lying."

18

"Naw, I ain't. It was a voice, I swear."

"I didn't hear nothing."

"Then stay here by yourself. I'm gone," Mitch said, running.

"I'm gone, too," called Beauford.

They ran and ran with Mitch holding onto the snake and his lunchbox and Beauford looking from the road back to the woods and to the road again, listening, running, listening.

They reached their house and Mitch burst through the back door.

Outside a hush fell from Mother Harriet's hill, the creaking porch swing, the distant hum of traffic. The Pee Dee ambled back to sleep, lowering its algae gums from the skipping, whistling stones that had been food upon the water. The river rose only slightly now, like a man tossing in sleep; but the stones were urging it to speak. The river opened its rippling lips and said, "Yes, boy. You coming back."

Harriet Henry turned to Addie Miller and spoke so quietly that Addie had to stretch her ears. "Lord, when Jake do come back, *we* gonna be the surprise. Ain't we, Jordan?"

"Jordan gone," said Addie.

"Gone? Where my boy gone?"

"There's my little man," said Maggie as Mitch pushed through the back door, almost colliding with Ruthie who was moving between steaming pots on the stove and filling up a plate.

"Look out, Mitch. I got to run before this food gets cold." And Ruthie was gone with the plate of dinner out the same flapping door.

"And where was you and Beauford, Mister Man? Not cleaning up Harriet's backyard like you supposed to," said Maggie, filling other plates at the stove.

"I found me a snake, Mama. A baby snake."

"Where's Beauford?"

"He outside."

"Ain't we got enough pets around here. Especially you, weasel."

"Aw, Mama."

"And I know you don't expect me to fix your dinner with that worm in here grinning at me. Naw, sir. Out he goes." And Maggie pointed her wiry fingers at the flapping screen door.

"Mama, it's just a baby. I'll take care of it."

Maggie watched the snake coil and uncoil about Mitch's open palm. "He might get taken for a sausage," Maggie warned. She laughed and Mitch laughed with her.

Jeremiah and Beauford came in from the toolshed.

"Honey, Mitch done caught himself a live sausage," said Maggie.

"An ugly looking one, too," said Jeremiah. He laughed with them and patted Mitch on the shoulders. Beauford stood by silently. Mitch beamed.

Ruthie knocked once at the door of the white planked house and walked right in. It was their signal. But instead of Harriet greeting her, she was being helped into bed. Ruthie put the covered plate on the night table and helped Addie turn down the quilts and sheets and prop two pillows up to hold Harriet's back. Then Harriet ate. She took the spinach leaf by leaf, the yams a half-forkful at a time, and the soft-boiled chicken muscle by muscle. Addie Miller started singing a church song without tapping her feet. "Just rest your nerves, honey," Addie said.

20

Ruthie left the house and ran down the hill.

Addie Miller waited to see if any spasms of rheumatism or grief would return. When nothing happened, she continued humming by Harriet's bed. Soon Mother Harriet was asleep. Her head leaned away from the half-eaten food. Addie took the plate into the kitchen, nibbling at the remaining bits of chicken as she went. She gathered her shawl and left the house without another word. She inched slowly down Harriet's driveway, tapping the hard clay with her cane and moving arm in arm with the coming night.

Ruthie got home just in time to hear Maggie's anger. "Mitch! Where are your shoes?"

The boy jumped in his seat at the table, unsure of Maggie's voice, but one look at grinning Beauford told him it was true. He was done for now. Would she whip him? Would Jeremiah? His father was silent, and that could mean anything.

"I don't know, Mama."

"What you mean you don't know?"

"When I was looking for them turtles at the Pee Dee, I guess I took them off at the road so I could wade in."

"What road?" asked Jeremiah.

"The road back to the Pee Dee," Beauford volunteered.

Mitch sank in his chair. Punishment was reaching for him. He could touch it.

"Highway 74," Beauford said.

"You boys know not to go near that highway, don't you?" said Jeremiah, taking over from Maggie. "Y'all know better than that."

"Pappa, you said we could go to the river sometime this spring. The schoolbus stops right there," said Beauford.

"I know I said it. But I meant when I take you. Just cause the bus stops there don't mean you got to get out and walk around down there like you home."

21

"But, Pappa," said Mitch.

"I ain't gonna tell you boys again."

"And you, Mister Man, you better find them shoes. Cause I ain't gon' all the way into Rockingham to buy no more," said Maggie, all in one breath. Her eyes found Jeremiah's as troubled as her own.

"It's all right," he said. But he was speaking to Maggie, not to Mitch, and Mitch knew something was wrong between them. His lost sneakers were to blame.

Maggie's wet, blinking eyes found Ruthie. "Mother Harriet eat all her food?"

"I don't know, Mama."

"What you mean you don't know?" said Jeremiah. "Why it is nobody knows nothing in this house?"

"Addie was putting Mother Harriet to bed," said Ruthie. "So I didn't see her finish."

"What she say?" asked Maggie. "She like my yams?"

"She didn't say nothing. She ate slow, like she couldn't even swallow. Addie said she was tired. And Mama, she didn't say nothing to me the whole time like she didn't know I was there."

Maggie turned to Jeremiah. "I thought you said she was up and about this morning?"

"Sure was, Maggie. Fussing and cussing around that house like a spring chicken. I'll stop by to see her in the morning."

"Why wait till morning?" asked Maggie. "Why not now?"

"In the morning," said Jeremiah, and that was that.

Later, Maggie and Ruthie cleaned the kitchen. Jeremiah and Beauford put tools away in the shed. Mitch found a used cigar box for his snake and filled it with wood chips and grass. He placed the box delicately under his bed. Ruthie and Beauford went quickly to sleep. Mitch tried to sleep, but he kept hearing Maggie and Jeremiah arguing in the next room. Maggie's voice came breathy and exhausted; it worried him. He got up from the bed and went into their room. Maggie's cheeks were wet.

"Mama, what's wrong?"

"Nothing, son. You go on back to bed."

"You sure, Mama?"

"Yes, son." Her voice was low again, different.

Jeremiah watched Mitch so intently that the boy felt uneasy in his cutoff pajamas. It was as if his father was seeing him for the first time. Mitch wasn't sure what his father saw. He stepped back from the bed.

"Mama, who's Jordan?"

"Who said anything about Jordan?" asked Jeremiah.

"When we was walking home, me and Beauford, I heard someone calling Jordan. Telling Jordan to come home. Who's Jordan?"

Maggie looked at Jeremiah, then back to Mitch. "He's an old friend, Mitch," she said. "From long ago."

"He live around here?"

"Naw, son."

"He any kin to us?"

"Why you ask that?" said Jeremiah.

"Cause it sounded like Mother Harriet calling him."

"Maybe," said Maggie. "Jordan was her grandson."

"Where he at now?"

"I guess he gone north. What you reckon, Jeremiah?"

"Guess so," said Jeremiah. Then his tone lightened. He almost smiled at Mitch. "Now, don't you think it's time you went back to sleep?"

"Yes, Pappa. Good night."

"Come give me some sugar before you go," said Maggie, leaning to kiss him.

"Good night, Mitch," said Jeremiah.

23

Mitch returned to bed beside Ruthie. He folded himself into her warm, sleeping shoulders. Beauford lay on another bed in the opposite corner, wheezing through his open mouth.

Mitch could still hear his parents. And he couldn't stop listening.

"I know how you feeling," Jeremiah was saying.

Maggie was spent of energy. "What does it mean?"

"I don't want to think about it like that, honey." Jeremiah turned off the light and moved closer to her. Maggie was still.

"Maggie," he said. "We got each other, baby. And the kids, too. Beautiful kids." He felt her breath low and even beside him, closer now for protection. He touched her thighs.

"It was so long ago."

"I know, Maggie."

"And now Mitch."

"Don't worry. It don't mean nothing."

"You sure?"

"The river's for everybody."

"You sure, Jeremiah?"

"Everybody, Maggie."

"I just hope Harriet ain't dragging my kids in it. It's her mess, not ours."

"Don't worry, baby."

Jeremiah eased himself upon her and Maggie felt warm. She opened for him slowly, too tired to share the pleasure but she allowed him his. He entered her with a dull thud and with each thud she sank deeper into the bed, deeper into sadness. She heard gravel drop onto a casket deep in the ground. *Pine wood,* the man in the black suit had said to Maggie and Mrs. Johnston, the only family left. *The best pine wood for the boy.*

24

Mason, Mitch. Mason. The names rolled together inside her. Maggie tried tossing and turning under Jeremiah's pressing body. Tears welling up inside her gave weight to the names and faces which she held until she almost choked. "He was . . . the only brother I ever had."

"But it's all right, now," Jeremiah said. "It's all right now." He tried telling her more with his pressing close, that she could work it out. Push it away from her if she tried. Push and push. But *thud* went another shovel of gravel, heavier on the pine wood, heavier on her pine knotted face.

"Maggie, it's me, baby. And I love you."

If she tried she could work it through. Push and work, push and work. *Thud.* The earth piled higher. *Thud.* Higher and heavier until it closed out the feeling in the pine wood of her face and thighs and until there was no more *thud* sounding on top and Maggie stirred cautiously lest Jeremiah touch where she would lose control over the pushing and working out, but before she know it he was so deep inside her that she could hear her own voice calling up and away from the pine creaking *Mason* with her own crying again, *Mason,* and moaning and crying until she was limp and whimpering, "Mason." Maggie shivered close to Jeremiah, his sweat glueing them. Maggie thought she was safe. *I am safe now from the pine wood and the names of the faces.* But Jeremiah continued to push and rock her away from those thoughts, away from memory with his pulsing chest and thighs, first quick and deep, steady to a peak, then calm like a fever fading.

2

In the middle of the night Mother Harriet awoke with a start. She pulled back the patchwork quilt and stretched her grainy hands upon the stark white bed sheets. Her throat was dry, her skin parched and cracked like drought-plagued soil. Her walnut wrinkled hands mirrored her face. Eighty years old with no family around to care for her, she was weakened by solitude and by the arthritis that periodically immobilized her. Whatever had awakened her in the dark this time happened some twenty-odd years ago. And Harriet Henry had no one to blame but herself.

They had been weeding the cornfield and clearing brush all day when Mother Harriet made Jordan chop extra firewood before supper. From the kitchen of their four-room house, she watched him swing the axe between his tired legs until it bit a wide vee into the wood, separating it. Jordan's firm stance and wide arching arms belied his thin, gawky thirteen-year-old body. Sweat beaded into his tight curly hair, ran down his face and neck. He was almost a man. Mother Harriet would see how strong he was, how hard he could work.

She left the kitchen and stood outside, studying him and the wood. Then she told him what else he could do with the axe, or with his bare hands. Jordan stopped chopping in midswing, his eyes and mouth open in disbelief.

"You hear what I say?" said Harriet.

"Don't ask me that, Gran'Mama."

"You hear what I say?"

When he didn't answer, the edge of her knuckles hit his

face. Through his tears Jordan said, "He's my Daddy, ain't he?"

At sixty Mother Harriet couldn't handle a shotgun well enough to take the perfect aim she would need. But she wasn't too old or too weak to make Jordan listen. Night and day she popped words at him like so much chicken feed, "Get him, son. Get him for me and for your Mama." Then pecked them off him bit by bit.

"He's my Daddy, ain't he?" Jordan said again.

"Then where he at, if he your Daddy?"

"Don't ask *me*, Gran'Mama."

"Boy, you don't even know what he look like."

"I saw him once."

"Well, I hope you saw him good enough to get."

"Don't ask me that."

"Boy, I ask you anything I want to." Her words gnawed at him, were teeth at his bones. She walked back across the porch and into the house. The screen door slammed shut.

From the kitchen wood stove, she watched him search the early evening sky. He looked at his hands already sore with calluses. He was strong and certainly no coward. He had cradled his friend Mason on the highway between Rockingham and Wadesboro just like Harriet alone had cradled him alive when he was born. But her words, more than the work she made him do, caused his whole body to ache.

Jordan took up the axe again and chopped until he had enough wood for Harriet's cooking the next day. She watched as he returned the axe to the toolshed, then walked with measured steps up onto the porch with wood high in his arms. He piled it neatly beside the screen door. Jordan searched the sky again and shrugged his shoulders.

27

He came in to supper.

Mother Harriet was smiling. "I didn't mean to get that angry, Jordan."

He said nothing.

"Why let that no count Jake come between you and me? He already done come between me and your Mama. You look just like her, Jordan. Just like Chloe."

"Yes, Gran'Mama."

"And look here. I fixed your favorite dessert. Peach preserves on biscuits. Want me to warm them up? The stove's still hot."

"I ain't that hungry, Gran'Mama."

"Don't be mad at me, boy. Please. It hurts my heart to see you angry at me."

Jordan finished his meal of stewbeef on rice, then pushed the dessert away. "I reckon I'm just too full."

"I seen you working. You even old enough to dip snuff. Want some? I think I have a little bit left."

"Naw, mam," said Jordan.

"Tastes like good dirt," said Harriet.

"Like grave dirt, Gran'Mama?"

Mother Harriet looked at Jordan without a word.

"You like grave dirt, don't you?" Jordan said and pushed back from the table. He reached for his jacket by the door, moving on energy from the work she made him do.

"Where you going?"

"Down the road a piece."

"Don't be long, Jordan. You ain't that grown yet."

"How grown I got to be, Gran'Mama?" he asked.

"Lord, Lord, Lord," said Mother Harriet. She held her head in her hands and leaned on the table. "It hurts my heart, just hurts my heart."

There was no mistaking Jordan's look. He was getting back at Mother Harriet for insisting that he see Chloe's

grave behind the Good Shepherd Baptist Church. She made
him not only touch the grave and pray, but stick his hand
deep in the soil until it stuck under his fingernails. "Promise me, Jordan, you won't forget her," Mother Harriet had
said. And Jordan had answered, "Yes, Gran'Mama, yes,
yes."

He had been too scared to say anything else. And his
fears were justified.

"You can eat this dirt, you know."

"Don't say that, Gran'Mama."

"Just taste it. You ain't got to swallow."

"But I promised, Gran'Mama. Ain't that enough?"

"Chloe didn't hear you."

"I promise, Chloe. Now can we go home?"

"Chloe was your Mama, boy. I ain't got no more
children."

"You have me, Gran'Mama."

"You sure, boy?"

"Sure, I'm sure."

"Hold my hand and say it."

He held her hand, a flesh net of bones like pebbles in
a beanbag, peas in a dried-up pod. She held on tighter.

And before he could turn away, Mother Harriet pinched
the red dirt and was putting it in her mouth, just enough
to coat her few remaining teeth. Jordan didn't know what
to do. His fear held him tighter than Harriet's grip. She
prayed again with her eyes closed. Slowly, his fingers eased
out of her grip; he brushed off his clothes and walked
quickly over the gravel path leading to the church driveway
and out to Route 145. Harriet had to walk the two miles
back alone, but she knew the path by heart.

The Henrys had farmed in Pee Dee longer than Harriet
could remember. She and Pa Henry, second cousins, had
married and stayed on to work the land after their siblings

29

dispersed to points north and west, looking for more land
to buy or rent than the whites there in Anson County were
willing to part with. Harriet and Pa Henry took over when
their folks died and made theirs the best farming this side
of the Carr Mountains. It seemed like everyone wanted
a piece of that land. Jeremiah, from down the way, who
married the Johnston girl, Maggie, after Mason was killed,
received a parcel out of sympathy and celebration. Then
the main road below the Henry property got paved and
named Route 145, the quickest way to Morven and South
Carolina just over the line. But long before Mason faced
those speeding headlights down Highway 74 crossing the
Pee Dee River, it was Jake Williams who surprised everyone
by courting Chloe and scheming to take over the farm as
if her family was the poor and irresponsible one, not his.
When Chloe was only sixteen and knew nothing about
men, Pa Henry's heart failed and Harriet had to finish raising the girl the best she could. Chloe didn't know much
about the lies young men would tell in their frenzy, and
she believed that the fireworks in Jake's talk were roadsigns to heaven. Mother Harriet would rather die than give
up land or family to Jake. Getting Chloe pregnant was
enough to earn Harriet's anger. But to walk out on Chloe
days before her water broke, so she had to inch her way
bowlegged up to Harriet's solitary hill by herself, turned
Harriet's anger into simple, cold hatred. Chloe's first shriek
of complicated labor was enough to cement the hatred into
vengeance and erect the single obsession of her life, no
matter how much longer she had to live. Years later, when
Jake showed up with a surprise wrapped in newspaper,
the burden was too much for Harriet to bear alone. Against
her better judgment, she told Jordan how Chloe died. Right
away, he started having nightmares. He had all but memo-
rized the scene. Mother Harriet's eyes were windows on

Jake and Chloe, first one, then the other until their sounds and faces frightened him awake, both in the telling and in his torturing sleep.

Chloe's cries peel from the ceiling of the room and slide out into the night.

"Aaaahhh. Aaaahhh."

Chloe sinks into delirium.

Jake leans against the outside of the house. He takes a swig of whiskey that keeps telling him to ignore the noise.

Chloe's forehead is covered with sweat. She clenches her teeth and pushes the mound of her belly. Contractions come fast and lock her thighs. Her moans fill the house, exit slowly. She takes a fast breath. The night outside holds as much of her pain as it can. The rest begs to be let back in.

Jake's head hunches forward into the folds of fat below his chest. "This sack's empty," he says to himself. "Not like hers, naw sir. Not like hers, pretty pecan."

The house fills with activity. Mother Harriet bends between Chloe's legs, and Addie Miller holds her open, steady. Harriet strokes the upper part of Chloe's belly, easing the mound down, down, down until the weight shifts unexpectedly and Chloe's screams cut the air. Blood spills from her. Her legs pulse feverishly. More blood. Too much. Harriet looks at Addie, says nothing, her lips hold hard against the trembling in her hands.

Jake tries to shake off the numbness growing all over him, from his flat broad nose to his cheek with the scar. Whiskey has the only power to move him. "I should be celebrating," he yells, but no one hears him. The wind sends his drunk breath right back in his face.

Harriet's eyes hook the other woman into her fear. They work to stop the bleeding, when a sudden hump of black and red pushes its way out and onto the sheet, coloring

31

it with new life, then fingering for food and light and touch.

"Whooee," Jake shouts, toasting the night with the green tinted bottle.

Chloe shakes in her fever and lets go.

"Aaaaahhh," sounds behind him. No echo, but someone somewhere calling into his head.

Mother Harriet knows the danger. She pulls the wet shape to her chest. It breathes, comes fully alive. Addie Miller loosens her hold on Chloe's limp legs. She fetches the kettle of hot water and helps Harriet clean the baby. Addie wraps it in a wool blanket. Harriet draws the sheet over her daughter's hips, shoulders, and head.

Jake holds his numb face against the increasing menace of whiskey and silence. Then the baby's crying.

Harriet's stomach tightens, eyes start to burn. And there lies Chloe, stillborn at seventeen.

Jake feels the scar on his face hurting now and his hands reach all around him for all that he has touched and burned. Somewhere he's heard a baby crying, somewhere a voice calling for Mama and Jesus and Mama again. Then he runs and keeps on running as fast as his drunk, stubby legs will let him, crashing and groping at the night.

The baby searches for something to suck. Air. In and out, in and out. With her eyes like bullets about to fire, Harriet calls out "Jordan" for the river Chloe has crossed.

She'd get Jake for this, or die trying.

"That man don't love you. Not like me. Not like Chloe woulda done living. You hear what I say?"

"Yes Gran'Mama. Oh yes, yes."

Mother Harriet disguised her plans as best she could by giving Jordan chores to do to make him strong: weeding and shucking corn, repairing the outhouse, smoking meat for winter, sharpening scythes and axes, fixing the yard pump, drawing gallons of water at a time, spreading lye in the outhouse pit, clearing brush, feeding fires in the stove and under the backyard washpot with a steady supply of split logs and kindling. Then they stopped him. Jordan was thirteen. Mother Harriet and Jeremiah came up with the gun.

"You handle a axe good. I seen you," said Harriet. "You can handle a gun."

"Naw, Gran'Mama."

Jeremiah held out Pa Henry's shotgun. He nodded to Jordan and to Harriet. "Take the gun, Jordan," he said. "You almost a man."

And Harriet said, "Take the gun, Jordan."

"Naw, Gran'Mama."

"It ain't loaded, boy," she said.

"We just want to see how you handle it," added Jeremiah.

Mother Harriet spoke softer, but her words were sharp. "He coming back. Jake's coming back one of these days, for sure. Now take the gun, Jordan. Take it."

Jordan took the gun.

Harriet's face cracked into a smile, "Good."

"Good," Jeremiah repeated. "Tomorrow, I'm-a show you how to take it apart, clean it, put it back together again, and shoot."

Mother Harriet grinned wider now. "Jake ain't gonna have no newspaper surprise this time."

"Naw, mam," said Jeremiah.

"We gonna be the surprise." Then she laughed, cackling and wheezing through her three remaining teeth.

Jeremiah laughed, too.

"We gonna be the surprise," Harriet said again. "Ain't we, Jordan? Chloe cut him, now you gonna finish it."

"Don't ask me that," said Jordan.

33

"Boy, you hear what I say?"

Jordan said nothing. The gun slipped through his hands and rested on the hard, red ground.

The next morning Mother Harriet rose with the sun and waited a good two hours before fixing breakfast. She thought about the night before and regretted Jeremiah's presence. He seemed to egg her on with Jordan, and now knew all her business. But it was Jordan who would inherit the land, not Jeremiah, no matter how eager he was to please. Who was Jeremiah anyway, but a neighbor's boy who wanted to help Pa Henry on the farm rather than finish the sixth grade? Jeremiah must have had his eyes on Chloe, too. It was suddenly clear to Harriet that Jeremiah's six-foot frame and beady eyes must have harbored just enough envy of Jake to match her hatred. His presence spurred her on with Jordan, made her ride him. Jeremiah had ideas about the land, too. And now Harriet had to free herself from Jake's threat of return and perhaps Jeremiah's interests, too. Jordan better learn how to shoot, she told herself. Maybe the surprise wouldn't be for Jake Williams alone.

She knocked at Jordan's door. "Got hot biscuits and molasses for breakfast, Jordan. Get up now." She listened for his stirring, his complaints, his pants slipping on, his belt snapping into place. Nothing came. Harriet pushed open the door and saw Jordan's quilts and sheets in disarray. But no Jordan. She looked in the toolshed, the outhouse, tapping the footpath brush with a stick to frighten away snakes. There was no Jordan. Then it hit her and knocked the wind right out of her chest. She grabbed her arms tight about her. "Help me, Jesus," she said in a near whisper, sucking in her words and teeth and bringing air back to her lungs. Then she half ran and hobbled and ran down the hill to Addie Miller's shack store. Still, no one.

She knocked loud at Addie's house behind the store and walked in.

Addie was fixing coffee and mumbling to herself. Her lips kept moving silently as Harriet told her what had happened. "You think he gone for good?" said Addie, her lips moving faster than her words.

"Lord, I hope not," said Harriet. Then she lowered her head to Addie's kitchen table and cried. Addie stroked her braided hair.

"Ain't my boy gon' come back? Ain't he?"

"Don't worry," said Addie. "We'll get him back."

"Lord, Lord, Lord," said Harriet, holding her stomach in. "We got to get him back."

Addie said she'd go herself down to Jeremiah's, then over to Lou Crenshaw's place by the main junction to see if anybody'd seen Jordan. Addie didn't even bother opening up her shack store.

Four weeks passed and there was still no word about Jordan. No one had seen him. Mother Harriet's arthritis came back with a fury. She had to draw her own pump water and could barely manage. She stayed away from church until the first Sunday following Jordan's disappearance when she joined Addie Miller in the row of folding chairs reserved for the elders. Instead of punctuating Rev. Franklin's sermons with her regular *Amen* and *Tell it* and *Preach,* she was quiet until the service was about to end.

Mother Harriet started singing. She lifted her thick alto from the front row and spread it around the ten rows of the congregation:

> Jesus keep me near the cross
> There's a precious fountain

Free to all a healing stream
Flows from Calvary's mountain.

Addie Miller and the other elders joined in with the chorus.
Everyone sang and tapped their feet and sang again:

In the cross, in the cross
Be my glory ever
Till my raptured soul shall find
Rest beyond the river.

The words and feet-tapping filled the tiny Good Shepherd
Baptist Church. Then Harriet stood up against a hardback
chair and told the congregation what was on her mind.

"Y'all know the Lord been good to me."

"Yes, He has," someone said.

"And done blessed me with seeing my boy Jordan grow
up," she continued.

"Yes, Lord," came another voice.

"And you know my boy does good. So I wants you to
pray for me, this morning. Pray for me."

"Sweet Jesus," said Addie, and touched her friend at
the waist.

"That the Lord shine down his light and follow that boy.
Follow him wherever he is, and into glory. Glory, I say.
Even if I done wrong, Lord. Keep him from falling by
the wayside. Cause, Lord, I don't even know where he is."

A hush fell over the assembly. The feet stopped tapping.

Rev. Franklin stood up. "Help her, Lord."

"Tell it," said Addie, holding tighter now at Harriet's
waist. Holding for comfort.

Harriet held herself tight. She couldn't shout if she
wanted to with this load on her heart. "The Lord's been
good to me, yes He has. I say, yes He has!"

Her voice cracked. Her heart seemed to move from its place. Something was working its way through.

"And pray, church, He always keep me near the cross. And do for Jordan, Lord—"

"Hmm hmmm."

"Help him, Jesus."

"—Cause I ain't got nobody else." And her eyes poured their overflowing lids into the gullies of her wrinkled face. Sounds inched forward from the back of the small church like waves about to pull her under, or buoy her up, she couldn't tell which just yet.

> Till my raptured soul shall find
> Rest beyond the river.

Addie started singing this time, and tapping her feet. The preacher's baritone joined her and a whirl of voices rose up, swallowing everything. Feet-tapping on the wood plank floor was the sound of rocks and sand in an undertow. People hummed. The words and rhythm of the song kept Harriet afloat. Then she started to tremble. She shook the back of the chair. "Lord," she called. "Lord, please don't let me die like this."

The church hushed again. Harriet Henry was telling too much. Addie tried to pull her back into her seat. Harriet stretched her neck up and hollered, "Lord, Lord. I didn't mean to drive him away. I didn't mean to. I just wanted him to come into his own, Lord."

Mother Harriet didn't shout, but hung her head defeated, humbled, waiting to be washed in His blood. And once a year for the next fifteen years, she would start the same song and say her piece. The preacher incorporated her testimony into the order of service. Harriet Henry had her very own altar call.

A sign of forgiveness, Harriet told herself, was the letter that arrived from Philadelphia after Jordan had been gone a year. The envelope, which she studied a long time before easing it open, had the Pee Dee town designation crossed out and Lilesville written in. They had changed the post office. Then she read the letter slowly, savoring the taste and texture of each word:

> *Dear Cousin Harriet,*
>
> *How glad we are to see your boy Jordan after all these years. He's such a fine boy. And so grown! We're glad you sent him North to go to school. We're glad to have him with us. It was some surprise, cause you know how badly Hollis and I wanted kids of our own. We're glad you sent Jordan. He reads a lot, almost like he's hungry to know all sorts of things. He's smart, too. You should be proud.*
>
> *Funny thing, though, he doesn't talk much. Won't say anything about you all when we ask him. He says, "Mother Harriet? She's fine." Well, I guess boys are like that these days. They may be quiet, but they're always thinking. Well, Harriet, you stay well and look after your health. Hope you have some help on the farm. Our prayers are with you.*
>
> *Love from me and Hollis,*
> *Bernice*

The best news was that Harriet knew where Jordan was, in good hands, if not her own. When Addie came to visit and sit on the front porch with her, Harriet told her about the letter, read it to her twice, and made her swear not to tell anyone, especially Jeremiah. Harriet would tell him herself when it was time.

"God works in his own way for true," said Addie.

The women rocked in the porch swing the whole afternoon.

The new post office wasn't the only change in Pee Dee. They put a concrete boat landing at the river and closed down the primary school for the larger one in Lilesville, six miles away by the Anson County schoolbus. The train that passed through once a week for passengers ended its run. Now a freight train chugged along loaded with pulpwood as the International Paper Company bought up any land that wasn't farmed. Rock companies came into the area to cut gravel from the ground. The peach processing plant reduced its staff of all but the locals, so folk stopped coming in from Rockingham. Then stores started to board up and rot slowly. Addie Miller cleared her shack store of penny candy, cookies by the five-cent bag, and the rusting Seven-Up sign. She stayed in her house now, except for daily walks up Harriet Henry's drive to watch more changes come to their little section of Route 145 where a green reflecting sign now pointed to Morven and to South Carolina just several odd miles away.

As Harriet grew older, the farm fell into disrepair. Jeremiah, married now with three kids, hung around the place doing what he could. In her mind, he expected more land someday. Hadn't he looked out for her these years of Jordan's absence? Hadn't she shown faith in him with the gift of a parcel of land? Hadn't he been like a son?

"You come stay with us," Maggie said when Harriet's health waned.

"Naw, chile."

"We'll take good care of you like we been doing," said Jeremiah. "You can't stay on this hill by yourself."

39

"Can, too," Harriet said.

But in her heart, she knew they were right. She held herself in against surrender. She couldn't leave yet. Jake was coming back. *And you won't be nowhere around,* he had said. She had promised Chloe she'd get him before she died. And with Jordan gone she wasn't sure how she'd do it. She'd have to get Jordan to get Jake. But the pain pricking up from her chest told her she had very little time left.

Seeing the boys return from fishing was a sign that gave her hope. There was still a chance that Jordan would come home. It was Jordan, wasn't it? At least she called him Jordan. Addie tapped her feet and said she was a mess, but Harriet didn't care. She had seen him, and she believed in what she saw.

When Addie left, nibbling at what was left of her dinner, Harriet gave herself over to dreams until she was startled awake. It was the pain again, mounting inside her as proof she was as old and worn as the Pee Dee hills themselves. She got out of her bed and hobbled out to the porch. The porch swing was creaking in the night wind, moving by itself. Talking. Harriet Henry talked back.

"If it weren't for Jake," she said to the pines and the river breeze. "Him and them tore up overalls and stank whiskey breath. If it weren't for Jake, Jordan would be here now."

Pain rocked her body, boring like acid. It too had something to say, as simple and as clean as a knife thrust: *"Get him."*

Then Mother Harriet knew why she was still standing on the porch, old as she was, listening and talking back at the creaking swing, the rustling pines, and the stars shining from the face of the night like stuck tears. Those sounds and the acidic boil from her stomach told her what she had always known: that the North was now something different, not the freedom that it used to be back then, not opportunity for those who had already left Pee Dee, not a promised land, but something awfully different against which she had to stand up in what was left of Pee Dee and vow to get Jordan back before all that was left to tell about or live would be lost in the age rings of the pines surrounding her or be taken in the river rushing below. In her mind, she heard Jake laughing at Chloe, laughing at Jordan, laughing at her and calling,

    Yad Yad Yad Yad Yad
    Yad Yad Yad Yad Yad

And now the pain and the laughter beat into her vindictively, almost choking her on the name that slipped through her toothless mouth, pulling her lips into the wrinkled chin as the voice inside her sang,

    Yad Yad Yad Yad Yad
    Jake Jake Jake Jake

I'll be back someday, woman. Shit, you won't be nowhere around. And she knew there was only one way to do it, to get him back and good, both of them. "We gonna be the surprise, ain't we Jordan?" She'd need all their help: Jeremiah, Addie, Maggie, the kids, too. Mother Harriet stopped the porch swing from moving. The creaking also stopped. And in that electricity of silence, she realized she wasn't alone. The pain had presence. Some invisible hand reached way down her throat and seized the whole left side of her, stiffening her leg and lung and arm. Like a zipper pulling up too-tight clothes, pain shot up her side. The numbing hand inside her squeezed and squeezed, and a tingling bolt of paralysis crushed her. She fell to the porch floor and couldn't move. Hours later, it seemed, she was able to crawl into the house and climb back into bed. Mother Harriet did not get up. Outside, the porch swing creaked.

3

Five times in twice as many years Jake Williams went to the Greyhound terminal in Charlotte and bought a one-way ticket to Pee Dee. He carried no baggage, only a brown paper bag that hid the pint of Old Grand-Dad he sipped during the two-hour ride out. By the time the bus reached Wadesboro for the change to local connections, Jake was usually too drunk to move from his seat and had to pay the driver the return fare. It wasn't that Jake feared continuing the journey, he told himself. He just didn't know what he'd have to face there, or whom. In his mind's eye, he saw Jordan waiting with outstretched arms, eager to receive him and the surprise wrapped in newspaper. As long as Jordan was on the farm, Jake had a point of reference, a mark on the land. He'd go all the way to Pee Dee someday. That would show Mother Harriet, all right. The whiskey was supposed to help. But Jake was usually sound asleep when the bus pulled back into Charlotte.

On the sixth trip out, the whiskey wasn't strong enough to keep him seated. He got off the bus and walked the two main streets of Wadesboro until he felt hungry. He found a home-cooking restaurant and had something to eat. He went back to the bus stop which was empty. While he waited, he watched the intersection where signs pointed six miles to Lilesville, seven to Pee Dee, twelve to Rockingham. Then the emptiness of the platform struck him.

There were no cars going anywhere. Jake looked about him at the intersection, then at his skimpy clothes, his aimless, spindling arms. He stood like a solitary streetlight with no traffic to direct. If it had been noon, one could

43

say that people were off having lunch. But it was two
o'clock, and the sun wasn't even hot. Jake looked back to
the home-cooking restaurant which had been noisy only
moments before. Now there was silence. The town had
other things to do.

His flat broad forehead felt as empty as the street.
Although he had just eaten he felt hollow inside. Jake was
completely alone at the intersection without cars, buses,
pedestrians, or any movement at all. Wadesboro was pressing its weight of place on him, measuring his vulnerabil-
ity. Not even a stray cat stirred into the streets.

Jake touched the scar above his lips. He resolved once
again to continue his journey. But the silence around him
diminished even the memory of Mother Harriet's nagging,
raspy voice. The persistent image of Jordan's wide, expectant eyes and open palms started to fade. The bus stop
grew lonelier where Jake stood. No buses for hours, maybe
days, it was so quiet. Then by minutes and degrees the
emptiness unfolded its meaning. In a wave of gathering
sound it came clear to Jake that the emptiness wasn't his,
but Jordan's. The boy wasn't in Pee Dee, hadn't been for
years. Time had changed more than Jake was willing to
admit until the silence struck him and made his singularity
so painful and abrupt. There was simply no need for him
to ride the bus any more.

It was several hours before Jake could get a bus back
to Charlotte. On the way he didn't drink or sleep. He
watched the roadsides carefully, looking this time for signs
to confirm his intuition. The two-lane road changed to a
four-lane highway; filling stations gave way to outhouses
behind tin roof shacks; clapboard houses led to the trimmed
rose bushes fronting the columned brick homes of the rich.
Jake thought about the time he left Pee Dee.

He had been sitting by a campfire in the pine woods

and staring into the flames under a half-eaten can of Campbell's Pork and Beans. The hatred between him and Mother Harriet had stung him like a hit from a switch he tried to snap out of her hands and crack across his knee. He searched the heat and the wavering yellow-orange flames for a hint of a safe destination. He took another drink from a green tinted bottle; it tasted foul. He poured the rest on the broken, burning wood and threw the bottle away.

Jake had no money to go north, but he was sure the fire would offer another direction, a distance he could travel to safely and unseen. He waited, fought off sleep and the chill from the pine forest. He waited and he waited. Soon the flames from the liquor-splashed wood died down to a single wick and even that had nothing to offer. "Aw the hell," he said aloud and stamped out the remaining coals. He straightened up. Woodsmoke clung to his overalls and his beady, woollen hair. He walked farther into the woods. Behind him a hiss whispered from the cooling ashes.

Jake walked all the way to Charlotte.

He didn't start roaming the city streets and jook joints until Christmas, and later rode the Wadesboro bus for the first time. Jake started hanging out on Beatties Ford Road with the janitors and work crews who tended grounds at Johnson C. Smith University. Since the black school was the only place hiring, Jake got a job. Snooky, another janitor, told him about a trip he had made to New Orleans and the woman who read palms at the Crazy Eights Club. "With no money and no woman," Snooky said, "you's nothing, man. You got to find yourself a way."

That summer Jake was laid off. With no ties to keep him in Charlotte, he packed a shoebox lunch of fried chicken and boarded a bus heading south. He didn't take another drink until he reached New Orleans, found himself a room, and headed straight for the Crazy Eights.

Jake spotted the red and green layered head cloth before he saw the woman's wide face with the high ridge of her lips or heard her bracelets jangling as she moved from barstool to barstool, laughing, showing off the gold in her teeth. Her laughter eased into a smile when her eyes met Jake's and held on. *"Eh bien Bon Dieu,"* she said in a rush. "What you know good?"

Jake heard a song of accents and spice lift from her tongue. "I ain't got no palm," he said, suddenly bashful. He dug his hands into his pockets, hiding the torn edges of his pants.

"You got hands, don't you?" she said. She sucked in her teeth. The gold flashed. She pulled his arm and the reluctant hand appeared, the knuckles gnarled, the center almost swollen. Jake dug his other hand deeper into the pocket. Her touch calmed him. He kept watching her mouth for the gold tooth to show again.

"You got a fat life line," she said. "But it's broken in two places."

Jake smiled through his crooked lips. He gently laid his other palm over hers.

"Maybe, I can help. My name's Zilie," she said.

"What kind of name is that?" he asked, almost stunned by her directness.

"That's short for Mam'Zilie," she smiled.

"Oh," said Jake. "I reckon you ain't from these parts either."

He bought her a beer and she forgot to charge him fifty cents.

The next night Jake was back at the Crazy Eights buying Mam'Zilie a barbeque dinner. He told her where he was from. She talked about Haiti and the "polices" that ran her out of town for root-doctoring. How she got to New Orleans, she didn't know. Just passing through, really.

46

Jake said he was passing through, too. Hadn't she ever heard of Pee Dee? No. They laughed, and Mam'Zilie showed off her gold tooth again. The third night at the bar, Jake got so drunk he started cursing some woman named Harriet whom nobody at the Crazy Eights knew. Then he fussed about a pretty pecan he had cracked but couldn't eat. One loud man said he preferred walnuts or nigger-toe nuts and if Jake didn't shut the fuck up he'd have *his* nuts. Mam'Zilie eased Jake away from the bar and walked him out back to her upstairs room where he cried like a baby and dug his broken fingernails into her cradling arms. She let him sleep beside her that night and the next. Later, they moved together to an apartment house and lived as husband and wife. Jake tried to keep Mam'Zilie grinning. The gold in her mouth made him feel rich.

Jake told Mam'Zilie about Chloe and the lonely bus rides to see Jordan. "My boy. What me and Chloe had. Chloe was my Carolina pecan. We had a boy." But just as he spoke, he remembered Chloe courting the sharp edge of metal.

"Well, la dee dah," said Mam'Zilie. She sucked in her teeth, tucked her greying hair under a blue cloth and dropped her jaw.

"So you got peoples," she said after a moment.

"Chloe's dead."

"That's the broken part. I seen it in your life line. Broke in two places."

"I reckon. She cut me for it, too." Jake made such a long face his scar shone like new leather.

"Ain't but one thing to do, *mon cher.*"

"What's that?"

"Let me make it sweet to you."

"How you gon' do that?"

47

Mam'Zilie took Jake's head in her wide hands, the bracelets jangling on her wrists. She kissed him right on the scar. He beamed through his slanted lips.

"But that's only one place, Mister Jake. You broke in two places, like I told you."

"Where's the other one?"

"Don't you know?"

Jake searched his memory and came up short. All he had to go on was the click of Harriet's rifle at his head, his stumbling over the newspaper surprise, and Chloe's cut that kept him hankering after the piece of his lip rotting where they had made love.

That bitch, Jake told himself.

"Ain't we in love?" Chloe had asked.

"Sure, baby."

"I mean Jake, you always said you gonna do right by me."

"And I means it, Chloe."

"You sure."

"Why you ask me that?"

"I wants to be sure, that's all. So I can tell my Mama just how happy I am."

"I'm happy too."

"You sure?"

"Why you got to ask me?"

"And we gonna get married?"

"Sure, baby. Soon as I gets me some money. I'm gonna build you a big house, sugar."

"All mine?"

"Yeah, you and me, sugar. You and me."

"And the baby's too?"

"The—"

"The baby, Jake."

"What baby?"

She could have waited, Jake thought. Waited until he had things better off. She could have let him explain how he wanted things to work. It would take time, that's all. Time. She didn't understand that. Time. He tried to tell her but she thought he'd leave her, knowing that Mother Harriet would rather die than have it known that Jake Williams had had Chloe like that and left her before they could get married, or even wanted to. Chloe knew he'd leave her.

"I was coming back," he had tried to say.

"And here I'm calling you. But you gone. Gone. Think you can have me like that and just leave? Run out?"

"I was doing it for us, Chloe."

"Us, huh? I'll show you who's *us*." Chloe had the knife and before he could stop her she slashed it across his face, leaving him red and nearly blind just to keep him from leaving her. But he fled anyway, hollering.

"You a broken man, *pou' vrai*," said Mam'Zilie. "And I can't fix but one part."

"Which part, baby?"

"Don't you know by now?"

Jake grinned, wider this time, beyond the stretch of the scar. He pried Mam'Zilie's mouth open with his tongue, tasted the gold in her mouth.

"The rest I got nothing to do with."

"You mean the boy? You seeing too much in it, Zilie."

"Maybe I am, and maybe I ain't."

Not a word more was said between them about Chloe or the boy until years later, when Jake had put in a good ten years as a groundsman at Dillard University. One April night Chloe stirred his memory as if to mock his new life. She lay stretched out on a grassy field. Her skin was pecan smooth with a tinge of red in the brown to match the color and texture of the ground. As Jake watched her and came

49

nearer, the blades of grass appeared sharp and stiff without a breeze to comb them, curl them, or brush them soft. Chloe lay still. She could not have been more than sixteen. But what was he doing there, an old man in a solitary field? A wind started up in whispers and lifted him until he hovered above her like a bird, his chest hard and feathery, his arms now wings stirring the air until the grass moved like waves of brushed hair. The girl's own braids fanned out from her head like the spokes of a wheel. Jake's wings were now delicate fingers caressing her face with gentle pleasure. She smiled at him. She touched his chest, and Jake became young. The soft flesh of his chin and stomach hardened to muscle. She smiled again. Their lips touched. His mouth found her neck and the soft tips of her breasts. She pulled him closer, deeper, and he started to ride her moving hips. Her arms held him tight and kept him circling and circling through her muscles drawing from him in slow deep arcs all the fluid inside him as her face glowed, filling up from the hunger of both their years. And he lifted inside her, stroking madly in the waters draining from them both. He went hard at first, then slow, then fast, and was lifting and falling back into her and the fields and back into himself again, lifting and falling deep and holding tight and tighter until he heard the click of a trigger on something about to explode at his head and sound *loud loud loud* like a dam of thunder breaking and drowning him in heat, and when he looked at the long grass again he saw grey smoke and the long greasy barrel of a shotgun as wide as a cannon's mouth from which heat and smoke were billowing out and pulling him off the girl who was brown like the earth against the green sweep of grass and the white bed of clouds. Suddenly, below him, he smelled the acrid odor of burning flesh and saw only the bones of her he had lain with. Accidentally, he touched the skull.

It turned to dust. He jumped up screaming and the sky smoldered into a storm above him and the bones as if they were locked inside someone's pulsing chest whose heart was hammering him like a cold iron, blood-rusty nail.

Jake awoke and felt about him on the bed. Mam'Zilie was snoring against the wall. He tried to sleep a little longer. The dream had a hold on him still, a finger's worth if not the whole hand as before. He got up and dressed slowly, trying to summon enough energy to leave for work. Mam'Zilie, sensing he was gone from the bed, got up too.

"Jake, was that you moaning last night?" she asked.

"Me? Naw, I wasn't moaning."

"You sure?"

"Look, I'm already late for work."

"I ain't holding you," she said, gathering herself into a robe. "But if you see Joetta, please don't tell her I'm here. I don't want her big fists pounding down the door."

"What for?"

"She come by yesterday when you was working. She start to crying and flapping her lips about her man Turé what got him a red-headed gal from next county. Anybody can see that man got better sense than to keep sniffing around the Louisiana hog she is. It's a shame the way she carries on."

"You give her powders."

"The red and the green. Traffic lights, chile, for my kind of loving."

"And a charm?"

"Naw. Didn't need one."

"I hope she paid you."

"You know I always get my money. Nothing but change, really. You go on to work. I'll take care of her," she said as Jake slipped out of the door.

Since her days at the Crazy Eights Mam'Zilie's palm

51

reading had grown into root-doctoring. Love quarrels, debts, sickness, enemies, whatever went wrong people came running and Mam'Zilie would wrap a rose-colored cloth around her head, consult the roots and dust to find the cure. For five dollars, she would offer a sachet of powder to flake about the front door; for ten, an herbal tea from her kitchen garden stock that eased rheumatism, headache, or just plain *mal de coeur*; for twenty she would consult the spirit world, be possessed, and search for the origin and remedy of the client's trouble. But the older she got the more uncertain were her cures.

Jake didn't get far from the house before he saw Joetta barreling down the street. She was over two hundred pounds and almost six feet. Her deep-set eyes were bits of coal struggling in the hill of her face to become diamonds. Her arms flapped wildly, her broad face turned in all directions to catch anyone watching her and laughing if they dared. Jake chuckled to himself and got out of her way. She tried to reach him with her eyes, but they were lost in all her angry flesh.

"Jake, where Mam'Zilie? She in there?"

"Don't knock too hard, Joetta. She still sleep," he lied.

"Shit, don't get me started. Don't get me started."

Joetta patted in her midriff, tucked her collar up, and climbed the few stairs with a quick hurt dignity. Someone had to answer for this outrage.

"Zilie! Zilie! I know you in there. Let me in. I ain't no run-around customer you can hide from. Zilie! Zilie!"

"I'm coming," sounded from inside. *"J'arrive, chérie!* Oh, it's you, Miss Joetta."

"Every bit of me, too. And don't come pulling that French shit on me. You 'posed to be my friend. What was in that stuff I bought last night?"

"Just my love mixtry, chile. Come on in and sit down.

You look like you been through the war." Mam'Zilie tried
to laugh but stopped when she noticed Joetta's open pouting
mouth.

"I done like you told me, Zilie. And I done right."

"Easy now. I don't want no trouble this early in the day."

Joetta softened her voice. "I fixed my hair, scrubbed my
teeth and cleaned my neck like you told me."

"Now don't start feeling sorry for yourself."

"And I poked my bosom up and went right over to Turé's.
I sprinkles the red dust in my hair like you told me."

"Ah, the dried blood of a moon-struck rabbit," said
Mam'Zilie.

Joetta's eyes went big; a film of mascara ran from the
corners. "And I puts the green around the door."

"Hmm. The crushed shell of a mother turtle," informed
Mam'Zilie.

"Well, honey, I ain't through knocking when the door
slam open and that nigger jumps out at me and knocks
me down. *Me!* Then he pull and grab at my clothes. My
red panties is so torn up I had to throw them out. And
he's a-humping me right there on the front room floor.
I ain't had no time to say, 'Howdy Mister Turé' or smile
and get romantic. Shoot, he up and finished like that. So
I calls after him, 'Turé, Turé, ain't you gonna kiss me
none?' And he look around like he seeing somebody else
and starts to working on me again. But this time he gets
himself a rope, Zilie. And he ties me down! Here I am
trying to get up, my clothes all torn, and he tying me down
like that. You see these marks on my arms?"

"Ooooh Jesus! Papa Legba! Erzilie!"

"Ain't none of them helped. Turé did me two more times
tied up like that. Zilie, my clothes is thrown all around
that place just like a storm hit. And honey my head starts
aching. So Turé gets up, still looking like he seeing some-

53

one else and not me what's lying there. He say he got to
have him some more woman. Like I ain't enough. So he
left me, just like that."

"Naw."

"Yes, he did. Left me naked and sore and tore up. He
walked out and ain't come back yet. It took me all night
to get myself loose. I slipped into my house before anyone
saw me, I hope. Zilie, love ain't like that. You done me
wrong. And now Turé got his stuff and every black and
yellow gal from here to Raleigh, what you bet? And what
I got? Nothing but my hair pulled every which way and
this red shit stuck to my scalp. What Harold's Beauty Parlor
gonna say? Laugh me right out of town."

"Now, Joetta," said Mam'Zilie. "Don't sit there and mess
up my armrest with all that crying. Just look at you. You
ain't even cleaned up. Makeup all over your face, hair all
knotty. *Mon Dieu!* You been in the war all right and got
trenched up!"

"Zilie, you gotta help me. You gotta."

"I said it weren't easy. I'm getting old. Too old, I can
see now."

"Zillllllllliiiiieeeeee—" Joetta wailed and wailed until
Mam'Zilie had to close all the windows.

"And all the time, Zilie, he was looking like it wasn't
me he was humping. Like it was somebody else."

Mam'Zilie paced the room. She couldn't just tell Joetta
to leave because then the whole neighborhood would know
her conjure and root-doctoring didn't work right anymore
and that she was losing her touch. She had to think. Joetta
continued to sulk in the armchair with her wet eyes staring dumbly.

"Tell you what, Joetta."

"Anything."

"But you got to promise not to tell nobody."

"Anything, Zilie."

"And I'm doing this for free on account of you my friend and you in need. I ain't done this in some time and I could be run out of town if word got out. I don't need to be run out of New Orleans too."

"Tell me, anything."

"I'm going to do a contact."

"A what?"

"I'm gonna contact the spirits. Find out what's wrong with that Turé. Maybe somebody else got roots on him, like that red-headed gal."

"You think so?"

"Get up, Joetta. We got work to do."

"Do I look all right?"

"It'll be mostly me. You carry a tune?"

"From here to there. Church choir alto and tambourine," she said proudly.

"You got anything of his. Anything he wears or something from his body?"

"I got some of his hair, when he asked me to braid it one night and I cut some of it off. He didn't even know," she said putting her hand to her mouth.

"Where is it?"

"In my Bible, of course."

"Well you come back this time tomorrow and bring it."

"The Bible?" said Joetta, about to cross herself.

"His hair, chile, some of his hair."

"Well, I hope it works this time," said Joetta, getting up to leave.

"Me, too. *Au revoir, chérie!*"

"Work that French, Zilie. Work it."

Jake came home tired. All day long tending the college grounds and classrooms, he thought about Chloe and the dream and Jordan's absence from Pee Dee. For years he had felt the joy of being free, but the pang of aimlessness kept surfacing unexpectedly. He and the pint of Old Grand-Dad had nothing else to look forward to. Jake became so absent-minded that once he cleaned the same history classroom twice. He realized it when he saw maps of Africa and the United States and a smaller one of the South. Pee Dee wasn't even on the map. With Jordan gone, too, it was as if Jake was without a past. He looked at his hands and studied the fat life line Mam'Zilie said was broken in two places. "I can heal one," she had said that time at the Crazy Eights. But she said nothing at all about the wide spider web of lines that marked him like the tributaries of a river reaching for the veins in his wrist.

That night he couldn't eat his dinner. Mam'Zilie had taken out her teeth and was munching on the soft boiled chicken with her jaws collapsed, lips wrinkled and rice falling from the corners of her mouth.

"What you looking in your plate so sad for? Can't you finish? It weren't that bad."

Jake said nothing.

"I said my *poulet-riz* weren't that bad. *I* ate it."

"It just keeps messing with me, Zilie, that's all."

"That chicken ain't done a thing."

"I'm talking about Lilesville, woman. When I left Pee Dee."

"Humph," said Mam'Zilie. "Pass me the bread."

"You can't eat no bread with your teeth out."

"They just soaking. I had to rest my jaw some."

"You should get yourself some new teeth."

"Ain't enough money. You know that."

"Yeah, money. If I had—"

"Jake, forget about Pee Dee and think about business or something. You been cleaning at that college long

56

enough to learn something about making money."

"And all I got to show for it is the sweat under my arm-pits, huh Zilie? I sure wouldn't mind moving out of here," he said watching her closely.

"Moving? Man, just listen to you! *Mon Dieu!*"

Jake leaned in closer, his eyes eager, almost hard. "Ain't you sick of this city?"

"Ain't that much city in New Orleans," said Mam'Zilie through her collapsed jaws. "All you got to do is walk two miles and you in the woods. There's a whole lot of country here. You just too lazy to look."

"I don't see you rushing out for no smoked ham."

Mam'Zilie shook her fork at him. "Listen, Jake. Like I ain't told you this a hundred times. I left Haiti because of the country. Small as it was, folks would always tell lies on you. Specially if you worked roots like I did. *Aide-moi, Legba!* But I did it cause my Mama did it and she learned it from her Mama. Then things got pretty bad out there. The government started watching us cause folks was say-ing the root doctors was causing all the fuss among the working peoples. So they come around arresting folk and putting some to hard labor way out in the cane fields where nobody could find them. That's where my father died. I got away to Miami, then New Orleans. Almost had trouble here too. But I'm doing the only thing I know how. I be damned if I'm gonna do white folks' laundry. And here you come talking about the country. Niggers and the country—"

"But we can go back now," Jake said, remembering a toolshed, smokehouse, gullies of red Carolina clay.

"The Islands is too far and we ain't got no money. I still have to see my peoples what needs me."

"But you old, Zilie. Old as me if you ain't ten years older."

57

"Shit, you crazy man. I can still dance up a storm. Grab me any man I wants. Just like the old days."

"Like you grabbed me?"

"*Oh là, Bon Dieu!* Like I gave you a place to sleep. You done growed on me like a sore I can't get rid of."

"You got your powders, your ointments. Closets full of cat teeth and chicken feathers."

"They works when I wants them to work, *aide-moi Legba.*"

"So you kept me," he said, his eyes starting to grin.

"You free to leave any time," Mam'Zilie said through her wet gums. She finished the last of the chicken and rice and left the table without another word. She went looking for her teeth, but where were they? First to the living room, then the parlor where she gave her readings. Next the bedroom, but no teeth. She looked again in the kitchen and there on the shelf above the sink was the set of pearly white teeth with a gold cap on one. She twisted them into her loose mouth until they were straight and hard and gleaming in place. Mam'Zilie turned to Jake still sitting at the table. She smiled wide.

"I feels better with my teeth in and my jaw all rested. But Jake, you sure is some crazy man. *Un nègre fou, fou, fou.* You know I ain't gonna let you go back to that wild place, Pee Dee or whatever they calls it. I needs you right here."

Later, in her dream, Mam'Zilie saw the house and the hill for herself. She also heard the click of a trigger. Her face tingled and her stomach knotted with cramps. She saw the planked house on the red clay hill, the back window open and showing a light bulb, a shadow moving, then standing still. Was it a man's shadow? A woman's? She heard someone breathing hard, then moaning, coughing, and a shuffling of feet. Someone lay sick. Mam'Zilie could smell the sickness like rubbing alcohol and taste its pungent varnish on her tongue. But the shadow, moving and blurring and coming clear as a human shape, kept its face indistinct. Its hands reached upwards until a light in Mam'Zilie's mind snapped out, dissolving the shadow and the house and the hill. When she looked up again it was morning and Jake was gone from the bed.

Catch him, she thought, and got up just as quick. See what else he knows.

"Woman," Jake said, swinging around, his eyes yellow and red from lack of sleep. "I done told you everything I know about that house and them folks. Don't be throwing it up in my face again."

"I ain't started throwing yet, Jake," Mam'Zilie answered, but the strength in Jake made her cautious.

"That's been years now, years. And I ain't for you trying to make me feel bad. I ain't got to answer to you or anybody else. That's all there was, Zilie. And I told you that a hundred times."

"I know what happened to Chloe, but what about the boy, Jake?"

"I don't know nothing."

"You sure?"

"He's gone, that's all. Nobody knows where he is."

"And that Harriet Henry? You afraid of her, I know."

"She told me never come back. That she'd kill me for it. I know she hates me till I die or she dies. But I done put all that out of my mind. I ain't got nothing more to do with them. Nothing."

"You still want to move out there?"

"I was just talking about the country when I'm too old to work, Zilie. I ain't gonna leave you." Jake squeezed her shoulders, his hands firm.

"It's all right Jake. I'm just a little worried this morn-

59

ing. And I got to see that chile, Joetta again. Damn. You go on to work, I'll be all right."

"Bring you something back on my way home?"

"Yeah, some Red Apple snuff."

"Woman, you out of your mind," Jake said laughing. And soon Mam'Zilie was laughing too.

Before Joetta came that afternoon Mam'Zilie closed all the shades and searched through her china closet for four candles she hadn't used in years. One pale blue, one rose, two white. She began humming softly to herself. When Joetta arrived with the tufts of hair, the hum had grown into a song circling the entire room.

Mam'Zilie arranged the candles on the table in a triangle with the rose colored one in the center. She took four squares of paper from another drawer and gave them to Joetta. "Write Turé's name on these two and slide them under the blue candle and the white ones."

"Like this?"

"Now write your name on this one and put it under the rose candle in the center."

"Like this?"

"*Oui, chérie*," said Mam'Zilie in a deep, raspy voice. Joetta looked worried.

Mam'Zilie seated herself opposite Joetta and rolled the tufts of hair into two balls. She placed them in the center of her palms face up and flat on the table. Joetta fixed her eyes on Mam'Zilie who said, "Put your hands on top of mine."

"Like this, Zilie?"

"Now close your eyes and hum with me."

The moment Joetta settled into the tune Mam'Zilie started swaying back and forth and rocking unsteadily. Her head went around and round, her eyes shut tight. Sweat

60

crept to the edge of her head cloth. Her breath started even and low, opening her mouth and throat to the candle flames, drawing in a message. Joetta hummed the words over and over, trying to contain the mystery of the table and the increasing volume of Mam'Zilie's voice. Suddenly Mam'Zilie's hand twitched. Joetta drew hers away. Mam'Zilie grabbed them and squeezed them into tight fists smothering the tufts of hair. Their humming grew into words:

> Tumba Walla Bumba Walla
> Turé Walla Turé
> Tumba Walla Bumba Walla
> Turé Walla Turé

They sang and they sang until the walls grew ears.
"Aaaahhh," said Mam'Zillie. "Aaaaahhh. Aaaahhh."
Joetta shook. What sound is that? *Like someone else he was seeing and not me, like someone else he was calling,* she thought.
And Mam'Zilie said, "Aaaaahhh. Aaaaahhh. Aaaahhh."
Good God, thought Joetta. *She with them spirits now. Talking spirit talk. Scaring me half to death. Why she got to squeeze my hands so tight?*
And they kept singing,

> Tumba Walla Bumba Walla
> Turé Walla Turé

From the candles came a vision of flame trees dotting a Caribbean island and a sea bluer than the sky. But why was Mam'Zilie here in her own country? Ah, yes. Turé was from the islands, too. Jamaica, not Haiti; not where the drums of hollowed trees pulsed through the ground, not where night made dreams talk and dead men move.

Then a wind stirred up and made the plastic window shades flap out of cadence. Joetta kept humming. Mam'Zilie started moving in her chair, shoulders hunching, chest knocking to a rhythm much deeper than their words:

Tumba Tumba Tumba Walla
Tumba Walla Tumba.

Why she got to act like that?
"Island, Walla, Island!"
I ain't from no islands. Born and raised here in Louisiana.
"Tambour à tam-tam, Tambour à tam-tam. Drumming drum drum drum."
That's the shade flapping, Zilie!
"Tambour à tam-tam. Aaaahhh. Aaaahhh. Aaaahhh."
Why she got to scream so loud and I don't know what she saying? Why she got to act like that? Scaring me half to death.
"Man. A black man comes. A big black man."
That Turé. I knew it was him coming. Now we cooking gal. Go on, Zilie. Work your stuff.
"New man. New black man coming."
Must be for me. Well, he better be fine!
Suddenly Mam'Zilie was with him on a boat crowded with passengers and leaving the island. The ocean gurgled and puckered up in wakes from the stern. The sun warmed her face. But she couldn't move. Her feet were wrapped in chains.
"Aaaahhh. Aaaahhh. Aaaahhh."
Where that new nigger go, Zilie? He's fine as can be, ain't he? Ain't he?
The deck of the boat broke apart, splintering under the weight of chains and passengers. Mam'Zilie separated from

the others. The wood fell away. Long planks in the water held her breathless and bobbing in the sea.

"Aaaahhh. Aaaahhh. Aaaahhh."

God damn, she sound mean. You hurting, Zilie?

Sweat creased Mam'Zilie's face. She fell forwards onto the table. Her throat let out a hiss as if her brain and head were shrinking uncontrollably.

Good God! She worn out.

Joetta tried to free her hands, but Mam'Zilie held tighter. "No, no." The voice and the strong wrinkled hands held Joetta still. "Black man coming. Land. Land."

And Mam'Zilie was standing atop a hill overlooking a sea of lush green fields. People were bending between rows of cotton and filling their sacks. Out of nowhere came a man galloping on a horse. He rode into the woods. A shot was fired. The people stood up and watched. The man returned with a dead body across his saddle. The people pointed at him and at Zilie, crying *yad yad yad yad yad*. Then silence. The people returned to their work. Mam'Zilie saw a house and walked away from the fields to the higher ground. The house was white-planked and filled with voices. From one open window near the back, Mam'Zilie peered in and saw a mattress pressed into the form of a bedridden body. The body of a woman. And the woman herself appeared. Mam'Zilie reached in and touched her. She was cold and ashen, her eyes like marbles. Mam'Zilie recognized the face. That's when she started to laugh.

What she got to laugh at? Where that new nigger go, Zilie? I wants my man back. The young black one. Don't need nothing tired and old as me.

"Ha, ha, Harriet," said Mam'Zilie. "You can't do nothing now. Ha, ha, Harriet. You dead now."

Who's Harriet? Turé's Mama?

63

"A man is coming. Coming up the hill."

Turé! I knowed he'd get there sometime. Don't trick me again, Zilie. Not like you ain't seeing what's me.

"A man. A knife. Death and danger!"

What, Zilie? What?

Mam'Zilie's laugh grew louder and louder until she was laughing hysterically. The table shook. Joetta stopped humming just as quick and opened her eyes. "Great Jesus! Zilie, is you all right?"

Mam'Zilie smiled dumbly. "Harriet," she said.

"What you say?"

"Blood of a woman. Blood of a man. Death and danger. Lord, I don't know who's gonna lose." Mam'Zilie's teeth shone in the candlelight with sweat and saliva dripping from her mouth. Her eyes stared open and blank like the headlights of a car gone mad.

Joetta pulled away from the table and the shrinking candles. "I'm getting you some water and opening these here blinds. Then I'm getting the hell out of here, Zilie, before I gets so messed up I can't sleep tonight."

When she returned from the kitchen, Mam'Zilie hadn't moved. Then her head swayed from one side to the other. The glass of water spilled onto the floor. Tears came and cascaded down Mam'Zilie's worn face. "I don't know who's gonna lose," she said. She clutched at Joetta and held on.

"It's all right, Zilie. I'm here. It's all right." Joetta led Mam'Zilie to Jake's armchair and set more water beside her. Without another word, Joetta went out the front door.

Hours later when Jake came home, Mam'Zilie told him that Harriet Henry was dead.

"You lying," said Jake.

Now it was Mam'Zilie's turn to fuss. "I may mess up now and again, Jake. But you know I never lies about what comes to me in a vision. Didn't I tell you what day was good for getting that raise?"

"Yeah."

"And didn't I help you kick that sickness without none of them doctor bills?"

"Yeah, yeah. All right, Zilie. Tell me about it."

"Well, Joetta was here crying over that man again. So I looks into the candles to see what was up. And there was Harriet. I knew her from what you said. But how she done dried up like a prune. I wouldn't be scared of nothing like that. What can she do?"

"And what happened?"

"Nothing. That's just it. She ain't moving, ain't looking. Just lying on that bed like a rock. So I reaches in and touch her and Papa Legba, she was cold as ice, I'm telling you. Then I had to get out of there quick, before I got stuck out there with that Joetta hollering, 'Turé Turé Turé' at me."

Jake stared into space as if he were seeing someone else, not Mam'Zilie or Harriet or himself younger then, but someone lying on the hill as clean and fresh and brown as new earth. Mam'Zilie went right on talking.

"I'm getting old, and it wears me out doing this spirit work. I could use some peaceful times myself. Don't you see, Jake? It looks right good to me."

Jake said nothing for a long moment. Then he looked right at Mam'Zilie. "What does it mean?"

"It means that the blasted woman is dead. That's all. And with the house empty and the boy gone years now, you and me can get that land."

"Is the boy gone? You mean Jordan?"

"Just like you told me, and now I seen it for myself."

"Where he go?"

"Now, I didn't see all that."

"And the land?"

"Your blood's in it, too. Ain't it?"

"Yeah," he said. But he felt uneasy. Almost nauseous. He went to the bathroom and spat several times into the sink. When he returned Mam'Zilie was pacing excitedly. Yeah, he said to himself. He believed it was true.

"You think I should go out there or something? I mean to be real sure?"

"The house is empty and got the smell of death at the door."

"The smell of death, huh?"

"Harriet's dead, Jake. Ain't you glad?"

"Yeah." Jake looked at Mam'Zilie closer this time. "Sure," he said. "Maybe we can have our farm after all." Then he smiled. "Come here you big juicy Mama."

"Aw Jake, I'm too old for that."

"Naw, you ain't. I'm the one who decides that, you hear?"

"Yes, baby. Sometimes you are."

The next day Jake called in sick to Buildings and Grounds at Dillard. He boarded the bus with one small vinyl suitcase and no bottle. Mam'Zilie kissed him goodbye on the scar, her favorite spot, and gave him a cat's claw for luck. Maybe the other folks in Pee Dee would have forgotten about all his troubles with Chloe and Harriet and the absence of his son. No one had seen Jordan in years or knew where he was. And Jake could get as much of the land as he wanted. He'd send for Mam'Zilie later. With a new house and a little farming, she could give up her conjure. Grow different roots. No one would know her and they could begin all over again. Just me and Zilie, Jake thought all night and half the next day. The express bus eased into Wadesboro. Jake got off smiling and changed for the local. He rode all the way into Pee Dee.

4

On a warm, late April afternoon the sky above Ephramville, Massachusetts was the clearest it had been throughout
winter. Jordan and his wife Phyllis drove out of the one-
commercial-street town and climbed the winding road to
Mount Greylock, the highest elevation in the state. The
road with its hairpin curves and sudden vistas had just been
opened to traffic. The two of them surveyed the budding
brush like expectant children cautious and thrilled their
first day at summer camp. They were among the first
seasonal visitors to the damp picnic grounds and the
Veterans Memorial Tower with the glass dome. Gone were
the fists of ice about the trees. Gone was the snow, the
gritty salt that turned the asphalt into sandpaper and made
driving a test of will. But lingering in the air was the cool
scent of evergreen.

Phyllis was driving, and that made Jordan nervous. She
hugged the single yellow line, but she drove fast. "Could
you slow down, honey, please," said Jordan.

"Am I driving too fast? Sorry."

Jordan reached under the passenger seat. His package
was safe. "Well, we're almost there," he said.

"I didn't think I was driving too fast," said Phyllis. With
her free hand she released her hair from her kerchief.
"You're nervous, that's all. Relax, honey. Doesn't that sun
feel good on you?"

"It feels real good." Jordan let his arm dangle out the
window. He watched Phyllis and the curving countryside,
both as brown as cinnamon toast. But she had sharp cheekbones and a chin Jordan often buttered with kisses. His

face was hot, and although he was only in his mid-thirties, he could feel the prick of age moles begin under his eyes. Soon he'd have the same arc of near freckles that Mother Harriet wore with such pride. Jordan was just a head taller than Phyllis, who could gauge his nervous excitement by his jittery Adam's apple or the sweat curling at his collar.

By the time they reached the summit of Mount Greylock, an altitude of close to four thousand feet, the sun had disappeared behind a ridge of mist. Phyllis parked the car and hurried to the picnic tables that looked dry. But they had brought no lunch. Jordan pulled from the passenger's seat two sturdy juice glasses and a surprise bottle of white wine he had wrapped in newspaper to keep the chill. Just then the sky lifted its curtain of misty gauze. People oohed and aahed over the view. Phyllis, her back to Jordan, her arms stretched wide, stepped close to the craggy mountain edge. Below them lay the matchbox houses of Ephramville and North Adams and Adams and the green valley floor nibbling at the rise of mountain.

"You see," said Phyllis, reaching for sky and hill, "there is life after Ephram."

Jordan approached stealthily, the juice glasses in the pockets of his tweed jacket, the wine wrapped in newspaper held behind his back.

"Can you see the college from there?"

"No, Jordan, I can't. And it's just as well."

Jordan would have grabbed her at the waist, but his hands were full. Instead he whispered into her hair, blowing his one word on her neck. "Surprise!" he said and produced the wine.

"Jordan, where did you get that?"

"Not so loud," Jordan said looking around conspiratorially. A sign read *No bottles. No unauthorized fires.* He unwrapped the wine and glasses and stuck the crumpled newspaper in his pocket.

"And Vouvray, too?" asked Phyllis. "What's the occasion? It can't be Mount Greylock?"

"Guess," said Jordan, filling their glasses and looking to be sure they couldn't be seen.

Phyllis gnawed the rim of her glass, then laughed into the wine, almost spilling it. "Is it my birthday? Am I forgetting something? Our anniversary?"

"No, but keep guessing."

"The end of classes in two weeks, that's it? No more papers to grade?"

"Close, Phyllis."

"Well, I give up. I'm never good at these games."

"My contract's been renewed," said Jordan, lifting his glass.

"You mean another year teaching history?"

"Three years."

"More luncheons, faculty teas, trustee dinners?"

"Aren't you happy for me," said Jordan. "For us?"

"Can't we celebrate something else. Are you sure it's not my birthday?"

Jordan frowned. Phyllis took his hand, grinned at him. "I'm just teasing, Jordan. Of course I'm happy for you."

"Then how about a kiss, huh?" And Jordan leaned over, reaching her lips first, then buttering her cinnamon chin.

"Pour up another drink, Jordan. Not too much. We have to drive back, you know."

"Drive back? I'm holding you hostage."

Dong, Dong, Dong echoed up from the valley floor. End of classes for the day at Ephram.

"Saved by the bell," said Jordan.

"My God, you can hear the damn thing all the way up

69

here. And just when I thought we were in the throes of romance."

"A toast then to romance."

"Let's drink to the view," said Phyllis.

"And to us?"

"To us."

"And to Ephram?"

"Now, Jordan. It's only a job," she said in a nasal whine, her nostrils flaring. She shook her hair away from her neck and let it fall upon her shoulders, all straight and thick without a hint of the permanent she got at the black beauty parlor in Albany, New York, the only one within a hundred miles of Ephramville.

"You have mountains like this down south?" Phyllis asked, her voice thick and mocking. "Way down upon the Sewanee River?"

"That's the Pee Dee, honey. P as in Phyllis."

"D as in down home?" she asked, her eyes sharpening, accusing.

"D for determination," Jordan said in his lecturing voice.

"Or defense," she added. "You're being defensive again."

"And you're after my ass, aren't you?" said Jordan.

The clouds returned, pulling a wet gauze back over the cut of sky. The sun turned into a grey disk. The sky lowered and smelled of rain.

"The view's gone," said Phyllis. "You mean we came all this way for a five minute show? Come back, sunshine. Go away, clouds."

"Listen to that apostrophe, folks," said Jordan. "You should be a poet, Phyllis."

"I *am* a poet, Jordan."

"Sorry, baby."

"Now you're making me depressed, Jordan. And the

view's gone. It's getting cold. Here, take your wine back."

"I'll finish yours. This is Vouvray, honey."

"And it's good, Jordan. Can we walk some?"

"To the tower?"

"Then home. It was a good idea to bring the wine, Jordan. I'm sorry I spoiled your fun. I'm glad you got reappointed, Jordan. I really am. Maybe in all this quiet I'll get more writing done. Maybe a novel or something."

"There, there. Let's kiss and make up."

"Love me, Jordan?"

"Yes, I love you. And you'll write what you can when you can. Our next toast will be to your book. Promise."

Jordan led Phyllis by the hand to the round stone tower. They entered the spacious gallery below and climbed the narrowing spiral staircase to the windowed dome at the top. When they reached it, huffing and puffing, there was nothing to see but clouds. A white wall of nothing. Their voices echoed, their breath could be seen in the residual winter air that had taken refuge inside the tower and now refused to leave.

Outside, it was colder than before. Jordan noticed puddles of water he had missed seeing. There were fewer cars in the parking lot. It was time to head home before the weather got worse. Jordan drove. On the winding road down, Phyllis caressed Jordan's knee as he held both hands on the steering wheel and inched his way around the hairpin curves and through much of the increasing fog. The car slowed to a crawl and seemed to groan against the white wall in front. Jordan followed another car closely, using the red taillights as a guide. But what if a skinny black boy crossed the road with his fishing pole and a string of flapping, curved-tail fish? Would he find the brakes fast enough? What about the blood and stinking scales on his hands? Jordan concentrated so hard on the thickening fog that he found himself remembering his own child voice and Mother Harriet's advice.

"That's the North Star. You ever get lost, boy, you just look up at it, hear. It tell you where north is."

"Uh huh."

"And you follow it to find your way home. You hear?"

"Yes, Gran'Mama."

"In slavery times, folks followed it to freedom."

"And they got free, Gran'Mama?"

"Sure did. Followed that star right cross the line."

"What happens when the stars ain't out, when you can't see them for the clouds or something."

"Then you feel your way by the tree moss, boy."

"Tree moss?"

"Moss grow on the north side of the tree."

"Golly, Gran'Mama. So when you know where north is, you know how to get free?"

"That's right, Jordan."

He settled in the porch swing, rocking back and forth and counting as many stars as he could.

An hour later Jordan and Phyllis were home. The fog they thought was just the peculiar, erratic Greylock weather had settled over Ephramville, dulling streetlights and blanketing the sound of the college chapel bell.

That night it rained and got so cold it was hard to imagine spring or swimming at Windsor Lake or taking long hikes along the Appalachian Trail. It rained and rained until fingers of ice formed on the trees and scratched at the windows. It was winter all over again. Jordan turned up the heat in the house.

"Shall we get a fire going?" he said. "I'll be cold tonight."

"I'll put on some tea."

"I'll get some wood. I may have to cut some."

"Can I help?" asked Phyllis. "I like the way you split logs."

"Legs, did you say?"

"I'll make some tea," said Phyllis and slipped into the kitchen.

Jordan crept up behind her and held her waist. "I'll be back for those legs."

The thick pine smell of split logs and kindling on the back porch and the sudden snow-like quiet brought back other sounds and stopped Jordan cold at the cord of broken wood.

"You handle a axe good, boy, I seen you."

"Don't ask me that Gran'Mama."

"Now you can handle a gun."

Her voice had chilled him then. And after she left him standing by the wood, he tried searching the sky, but there were no stars. He'd have to wait. He went in to his supper of stewbeef on rice, pushed the dessert away, and reached for his jacket by the screen door.

"Where you going?"

"Down the road a piece."

He had measured his steps from the porch to the crest of the red dirt driveway going down. Then he let himself go. He ran without taking a breath or looking back, trying to shake off Mother Harriet's anger, brush off the seeds and chicken feed she threw at him and bury them underfoot. He skipped over gullies and dips in the road until he reached the tongue of asphalt that circled the Pee Dee River, as brown and restless as he. But what would it answer if Jordan could finally get the words unclogged from his throat, stuck seeds that tightened his jaws, *want me to kill my own Daddy,* as if the river knew nothing about death and loss and fast travel in the night, as if it couldn't hear him or talk back?

Breathless and sweating, Jordan reached the gurgling water. But his heart kept pounding and blocking out sound. He felt hollow. Empty even after all that food. He felt eaten through and through with Harriet Henry's hate. *Want me to get him. Get my own Daddy.* The river hushed its gurgle, stopped insects feeding from its concentric, smiling ripples. Jordan splashed water on his face, then poured handfuls of the cool metallic taste into his throat, over his head. His sweat washed free and his body cooled. His heart stopped pounding. Jordan tried to think of what he should do.

"Why she ask me that?"

The river gurgled and belched.

"She say I can handle a gun. What do I know about guns?"

Ripples lapped the narrow shore like tongues of different lengths, leaving foam like spittle on a bristling whizz of sand.

"What do I even know about him? Only seen him once."

The tongues drew back, swallowing themselves in silence.

"Mason would know what to do."

The lips, ears, and tongues of the river closed.

"What does she mean, asking me something like that?"

"*Hhhhuuuusssshhhhh,*" said the curl of water on gravel.

Jordan looked again for the star and couldn't find it. He went back home.

"You part of the earth, too," Mother Harriet said. But the time she almost made him eat dirt told him that something else was wrong. He wasn't old enough yet to make any sense out of Harriet's grief. The only reason

he went with her to the cemetery was to stay out later at
Mason's house, spend the night there more often. But he
didn't think she'd try to make him eat the dirt, not really
put it in his mouth. He slipped his hand out of her grip
and left her praying alone at Chloe's grave. Jordan went
straight to Mason's house and told him what had happened.
Mason laughed that high thin laugh of his and threw his
skinny arm around Jordan's shoulder. What could be so
funny?

"You ain't no Mama's boy, is you?"

"Naw, Mase."

"Ain't no fraidy cat, is you?"

"Naw."

"Can you jump a gully?"

"Yep."

"Can you skin a snake?"

"Yeech."

"Tie a junebug to a string?"

"Yep."

"Then ain't nothing to worry about."

"Huh?"

"Everybody eats a little dirt. My pappa say it helps the
system. And Mother Harriet got an old system."

"You can say that again."

Mason stood taller than Jordan by a good twelve inches,
but was just as skinny. He had knots in his hair like BBs
and his lips were darker than his skin and always falling
open as if he was about to say something urgent. His large
eyes carried more news than his words, and Jordan was
eager to listen. Although Jordan could make fun of Mason's
crooked teeth, he never did. Mason was his only friend.

"So let's tie up some junebugs and make them fly."

"Not by my house. Gran'Mama's still crazy. She'd scare
you, too, if you let her."

75

"She gonna want to know where you are."

"Can I sleep over?"

"Sure Jordan."

"I ain't no fraidy cat. I just don't know what she wants from me."

"Nothing, probably. When we gonna chase them junebugs?"

"Now, you want to."

"Jordan! Jordan, are you all right? Hurry up with that wood. It's freezing in here."

Phyllis's voice brought him back from Pee Dee. It was the same clear, enunciating voice that found him in the university library researching a term paper. Phyllis had come upon Jordan reading by the open door to his carrel. He had his own library within the library, not just a desk, but a locked door, one of the few such carrels reserved for honors students. Phyllis said she was looking for a book on the French Revolution and asked Jordan about it. His books were all on colonial New England and he laughed at her error in this part of the library. She came back to visit him again and again, disturbing his research, but giving him a good reason to be there reading, note-taking, writing until she would show up and they would leave for a beer at the campus pub. Jordan loved history. Phyllis was wild about literature. They started reading to each other aloud until late at night. Once, she recited one of her poems to him. Jordan kissed her for the rhyme in her voice, then probed for images left on her tongue.

"Jordan?"

Phyllis stood in the porch doorway with a cup of steaming tea. "Aren't you bringing in the wood?"

76

"Sorry, I guess I got distracted," Jordan said, piling the wood in his arms and following Phyllis inside.

"What shapely logs you have," she said, smiling.

"You're really after my ass, now."

The next night Mother Harriet's voice found him again. Loud, menacing, the scratchy sound of it, full of phlegm and ache and cold, kept Jordan awake. Phyllis stirred next to him. Jordan rolled away. He eased out of the bed. He went to the living room and stood at the front window, staring at the black formless night, daring it to come alive. It did.

"That man don't love you. Ain't never loved you. You hear what I say?"

"Don't ask me that, Gran'Mama."

Then Mason came into his mind and kept Harriet's strength at bay, for it was Mason who had said, "Never mind Mother Harriet till you grown." And Mason told him about a river inside him he could follow away from there. "All men get it. You get it when you as old as me. You don't need no star, just rub the tree moss you got growing between your legs."

"Tree moss between my legs?"

"You ain't nothing but a little guy, huh?" said Mason another night he slept over at Jordan's.

"I'm ten already."

"I'm fourteen. You got to be fourteen for tree moss. You got peach fuzz on your balls?"

"Naw."

"You got jism in your peter?"

"Naw."

"You got rocks in your throat, make your voice heavy?"

"Naw."

"Then wait till you old as me."

77

Jordan laughed. He thought about the peach trees behind Jeremiah's house and the peach processing plant where Jordan and Mother Harriet got leftovers for canning. But peach fuzz on a boy? Tree moss between your legs?

"You lying," said Jordan.

"Your peter's gonna grow big like mine. And you gonna have a wet dream, too."

"A wet dream?"

"Sure, to let you know you got the river inside."

"Then I can always take it with me," said Jordan.

"Ain't got no choice," said Mason.

"And never get scared or lost or nothing?"

"Yep."

"And get away from Mother Harriet?"

"Yep."

And Jordan imagined himself brown and wide and muscular with age. A liquid coursing inside him, more nourishing than blood. Liquid that would splash and foam, run ripples all through him when he wanted it to, or as Mason said, when he got himself hard as a tree trunk or taproot.

"When am I gonna get it?" he asked.

"When you get old as me," said Mason.

"Why I got to wait that long."

"Cause it takes time."

Jordan didn't believe him. "What does it look like?"

"Well, it ain't like water. Not really. It's white like clean spit."

"Now I know you lying, Mason."

"You wanna see mine. If I pull real hard I bet I can make it come out. It came out once in my dream."

"Where you get all this from?"

"My Daddy told me. Plus I had the dream."

"I ain't got no Daddy. Will I still get the dream?"

"You ask Jeremiah. Bet he'd tell you, you don't believe me."

"Let me see you try."

Mason rubbed his penis until it was hard. He pulled it fast between his fist and faster until his eyelids drooped and his breath came short. Just then Mother Harriet's footsteps sounded outside the bedroom door.

"Ain't you boys sleep yet? What you all doing in there?"

"We sleep," said Jordan.

"Y'all better be. Jordan, you still got your morning chores to do."

"Yes, mam."

"Mason? You all right?"

"He sleep," said Jordan.

The footsteps backed away from the door.

Mason was silently and quickly pulling on himself until he whispered in a panic, his mouth gasping for air. "Give me something to wipe on, quick. Quick, Jordan, anything."

Jordan reached by his pillow for the rag he used as a handkerchief. Then he saw it, liquid chalk covering Mason's fist, long gooey pearl-colored drops smelling of limes. Jordan gave Mason the cloth. Mason fell back upon the bed. "See I told you so." And just as quickly, Mason was asleep.

Jordan stayed awake longer. He fell asleep counting the years before he'd have his own water. The next morning, he hid the soiled cloth beneath his mattress.

Then Mason and his fish were crushed under the wheels of a speeding car. For weeks, Jordan stayed away from the river, away from the broad highway streaked with blood like a hit-and-run sunset. Jordan couldn't sleep then, and he tossed all night and prayed for God to bring Mason back or send him a wet dream for his own getaway. Let the river inside him rise up and carry him away, too. He told Mother

79

Harriet that he missed Mason, and he heard for the first time her voice of nails, beating Mason's pine coffin further into the ground. Her voice scared him more than his sudden loneliness.

"I loved Mason, Gran'Mama. I really did."

"I know son. Come out to the porch and rest your nerves."

Jordan followed her and sat in the porch swing, rocking back and forth, back and forth.

"Gran'Mama, it's like my stomach and all my insides got no bottom. Things just move through me. They don't settle no more. Is that how it feels to lose somebody? Somebody you love?"

"Well, now you know, son. I'm sorry you had to learn it this way."

Jordan stopped swinging and went to Mother Harriet.

"Hold me, Gran'Mama. Hold me."

"Naw, boy. You ten years old now."

"Gran'Mama, I'm cold. I'm scared. Please hold me."

"Naw, boy. You just stand there and feel it. Feel it good, Jordan."

"Please, Gran'Mama."

Mother Harriet turned away from him and walked back into the house. "We need more pump water, Jordan."

He plied the rickety, rusty pump until his arms were sore. Finally he leaned against the cold metal and cried.

Later, before bed, Mother Harriet came into his room. "Now you know what I been feeling. You know it good now, huh? But I'm gonna see how good you know it, boy."

"What do you mean, Gran'Mama?"

"You think your grandmother is nothing but love and Thanksgiving? And all you got to do is go over the river and through the woods, huh? Well, I got news for you. You can't love somebody till you learn about hate, chile.

80

And if you don't know that, you in for some real trouble. You don't even know who you are."

"I'm Jordan."

"Well, you gonna know soon enough." She closed the door quietly and left.

Jordan reached under the mattress and pulled out the soiled handkerchief. He placed it on the pillow. "I'm Jordan," he said, and slept with his lips apart.

For years thereafter he saw himself tied to a fence post before a blurring picture of a dirty man in overalls arguing with Mother Harriet at the clothesline. The man approached him. With his callused hands he fumbled with a surprise wrapped in newspaper. Jordan smiled, "Thank you. Thank you, Daddy." The man didn't go away, but turned to Harriet and said, "I'll be back one day. And you won't be nowhere around." Then it was Jeremiah and Harriet stopping him in the fields.

"Take the gun, Jordan."

"Don't ask me that."

"I'm talking to you, boy. Take the gun."

Jordan took it, held it in his hands slippery with sweat. The smoky, oily smell of the gun barrel was nauseating.

"You hear what I say?"

"Yes, Gran'Mama. Yes, yes."

And as Jake was reaching for him with the surprise wrapped in newspaper, Jordan pulled the shotgun from behind him and fired.

Jordan's whole body had changed. His voice had deepened, the ridge of his upper lip grew hair and a softer fuzz crept into his groin and stayed. His balls ached to be released, and when the veined taproot throbbed one early morning and sent its flow onto the bed sheets and pajamas, Jordan felt pleasure and terror at the same time. He wiped himself dry with the cloth Mason had used.

81

He was almost a man. He could go wherever the river led. He would study roadsigns leading from the highway stained with fish and Mason's blood, from the hills of Harriet Henry's solid hate, from the turbulent waters of the Pee Dee Jordan did not understand. He would study different places and persons and dates and decrees: 1619, 1831, 1954 and Toussaint and Napoleon, Abe Lincoln and Booker T. Washington. Men who traveled, moved rivers, fought back like the Indians who stood on the banks of the Yadkin hundreds of years ago and yelled to the white settlers, "Come on over and fight."

He'd fight. He'd fire the gun. Wasn't that what Harriet wanted? He'd take the gun.

But Jordan found he wasn't tied to the fence post after all. It was the porch swing that kept him rocking back and forth, back and forth. Should he listen to the woman who saved him, or protect the man who made him? What would Mason have done in his place? Follow the river, but which river? And what could Jordan do now, alone?

From the porch swing he counted up to fifty stars and wrapped himself in a net of constellations: Orion, Pegasus, the Little Dipper, the Big Dipper, and, there it was, the North Star.

It was shimmering in the night just for him.

Jordan went to his room, found underwear, three shirts, and a pair of dungarees. He reached under the mattress for the soiled handkerchief crinkled with Mason's smell and his. He took that too. Mother Harriet was singing by the kitchen stove so loud and joyously that she didn't hear him slip out the back door and down the red dirt drive. When he reached Highway 74, he put out his thumb. He kept his eye on the star. All the constellations lit up, it seemed, so motorists could see him. A car stopped. The solitary black driver was heading for Raleigh. "That's north enough to start," Jordan said. Before he got in, he placed the handkerchief very gently on the ground.

By dawn the hard, icy rain in Ephramville had become a drizzle. As the grey light filtered into the house, Jordan returned to the bedroom and to Phyllis's sleeping body. He curled up next to her and kissed the back of her neck. He felt safe and alert as if he had slept all night. He brushed the thick waves of her hair, kissed her again. She turned to him, still in sleep, but slowly, ever so slowly, awakening to his touch. He lapped at her firm, cinnamon body. She made incomprehensible sounds. He continued lapping, even when he reached the full dam between her thighs, rousing it from sleep and bringing it slowly to the breakwater shoals where he was paddling now, calmly, smoothly moving upstream.

Dong, Dong, Dong.
The chapel bell ushered Jordan to class and Phyllis to her writing desk. The rain had left huge puddles in the walk between Jordan's house and the faculty offices in Robertson Hall and along the way to the classrooms where Jordan would lecture. The monogrammed calfskin briefcase Phyllis gave him last Christmas slammed against his legs as he hurried to class. His shoes squished with water, and at the close of the lecture hour, Jordan found himself standing in a pool of rainwater and flecks of soil below the podium. His clothes were still damp. His tweed jacket smelled of sheep.

When he returned home that afternoon, Phyllis was out jogging at the indoor track. Jordan took a long, warm bath. Later he set the table, made salad, and had steaks ready to broil.

"It must be my birthday," said Phyllis when she saw the table. "I can never remember dates."

"Maybe it's my birthday," said Jordan.

"Jordan, you should have told me, given me a hint or something. Let me at least change clothes."

While Phyllis was gone, Jordan grilled the meat and hung Phyllis's apron back on the refrigerator door.

At Ephram, Jordan had come halfway around a broken circle. North had led him straight to cousin Bernice and Hollis's house in Philadelphia, a scholarship from an enterprising white lawyer to his alma mater, Groton, where Jordan was expected to bring honors to the fledgling basketball team or at least be musical or entertaining in the class play. Then it was off to Harvard where Jordan met the struggling poet who was to become his wife. Jordan graduated with honors in American colonial history and stayed on for graduate school, fortified with the names of people and places, wars, movements and decrees, dates and debates that gave him a past he could pass on to others, not one that made him ashamed and afraid to cross deep rivers into camp ground or freeze in the path of a speeding car, *honk, honk.*

Dong, Dong, Dong.

The chapel bell was a neat beginning and end to his classes. But if he ever stopped teaching for just a day and walked down the one main street in Ephramville and saw how deeply grained and historical were the bemused gazes of the townspeople, he'd know that even they had only recently come to tolerate his presence. When school was not in session, Jordan simply did not belong there. The townspeople, who resented the college that named them, achieved one short-lived triumph long ago when one or two landlords rented rooms to three "colored boys" who were admitted to the college under the cloak of light complexion, then were denied dormitory space because of "sudden" overcrowding.

Decades later Jordan Henry was welcomed with a handshake from Ephram's president. No matter that they had no other black faculty members in his division or department. It was difficult, wasn't it, to find the truly qualified? They found Jordan, who had learned history so well he believed it. Why, he had made it to Ephram College, hadn't he? Miles away from the gravel pits and peach processing plants, the paper companies tearing through the timberland of Lilesville and Pee Dee. History got him this far away. He was proud. He was safe, and he was qualified.

The week before the end of spring term, however, Jordan still had trouble sleeping. He heard the trees rustle with messages, and it dawned on him with a choking urgency that he was no longer in Cambridge where he was anonymous and free, but in rural New England which had its own rivers and hills to cross: the Housatonic, the Connecticut River, the Mohawk Trail, Mount Greylock with its terrifying hairpin turns and glass-domed memorial tower usually cataracted with fog. In one dream Jordan was walking toward a hairpin turn. A car was aiming straight for him. He gasped when he saw Mother Harriet in the driver's seat. "Boy, ain't you coming back?" He awoke to the chapel bell sounding the first hour of classes.

"Jordan, I'm tired of you tossing in that bed all night," said Phyllis. "You scare me and I can never get back to sleep. Please take some Valium or something."

"I'm sorry. I guess I'm edgy and restless lately. And now I've got to run."

"There you go being busy."

"I'm probably late already. Has the bell rung?"

"I haven't heard anything. Here, have some juice. You

should eat right, if you're going to rush all over the place."

"The bell will be ringing again soon. I have to run."

"But you've barely finished your coffee."

"I'll get some at the office after class."

"What about your Danish?"

"You can have it."

"Thanks a whole lot." Phyllis sank into the kitchen chair. Jordan snapped shut his briefcase and grabbed his jacket. "You're becoming impossible, Jordan."

He stopped and looked long in her face. Her eyes were wide and slanted at the ends like an Oriental's, her skin just a tone darker. Her hair fanned out from a single center part in her head and hung in great waves to her shoulders. Against Jordan's thinning curly hair and broad face, Phyllis looked several years younger although they were the same age. Jordan was developing a paunch. Phyllis stayed trim with afternoon jogging and cycling in the hills.

"You never ask about my days anymore, Jordan." She tried to tease him with her eyes, at least to make him smile.

"I'm sorry, Phyllis. I'm too preoccupied with finishing the term."

"Well, the Faculty Wives Association is having an afternoon *tea*." The word stretched wide in her mouth. "And I must put on my afternoon faculty tea face and be nice Mrs. Jordan Henry, B.A., M.A. and what comes next?"

"No jokes this morning."

"I was never good at abbreviations."

"Oh you do all right when you want to."

"What's that supposed to mean?"

Jordan said nothing.

Just as he was leaving, Phyllis stepped in front of him. She lifted her face and brushed strands of hair from her eyes. "Give me a kiss first?"

"You haven't brushed your teeth yet," he laughed. "And I've got to run."

"Jordan!"

He eased the front door shut and scampered away into the wide campus green. There was no wet grass or puddles to avoid, this time. Alone, Phyllis finished her breakfast and went back to sleep. The house was empty, quiet now.

An hour later she went to her writing desk. Ever since her success in freshman English at college, she had wanted to be a writer and had taken every literature class she could. Her teachers were encouraging, and she even won a few undergraduate prizes. Her parents, however, wanted her to join the family's legal practice and openly expressed their annoyance at having provided her with an Ivy League education, not to mention the private schools, just for her to become a writer. Her father, Amos Whitehead, the most prominent black lawyer in Boston and from one of the oldest families, was most adamant about Phyllis joining the family firm. But Phyllis declined, saying she hadn't been able to read the lease for her apartment. Legal language offended her. She wanted clear, hard images that moved on the page. They asked for proof, so every time one of Phyllis's poems was published in a literary magazine she'd send a copy home. But no one ever discussed them. And when she asked, her mother said "Dear, that's so nice. But it doesn't rhyme, and I don't know what it means." Her father said nothing. He didn't even smile. But one day he had to come to the police station to get Phyllis and comfort her when she pressed charges against a man who followed her through the Fenway that afternoon and tackled her to the ground. Phyllis never wrote about that. Her father's stare and her mother's silence to avoid scandal were more shocking than the attempted rape. They had little to say to one another until the day Phyllis brought Jordan home for dinner. And now Jordan, too, was busy, busy, busy.

These thoughts and Jordan's dismissive behavior were all of a piece, Phyllis concluded. They kept her from writing. She watched the morning stagger into afternoon and listened as a breeze transformed the spring leaves into hands clapping at the window. Phyllis remembered the danger in Jordan's sleep and her own restlessness. Whatever it was that came in the night seemed ready to stay a while. "Like something rooted, something hard," she said aloud. Phyllis tried to dismiss the noisy, reaching leaves. Her writing paper was blank. "Hard," she said. She bit the tip of her pen and wrote *tree,* thinking oak, elm, sycamore, white ash and elm. Tree rhymed with tea. She remembered the Faculty Wives Association and got ready to go. The white page remained flat and blank and empty upon the desk.

Later that night she returned to her writing desk while Jordan corrected papers in his study. "Tree," she said again to herself, then wrote in a flourish of energy and rhyme:

> Corner seeds and scratch the sky
> nest a bird and help him fly
> Tree, how still and strong to me
> Your root of pain and misery.

"Tree," she said again. Oak, white ash, elm. *Your root of pain and misery.* And she imagined the bark of the black man's body following her. How she clawed at it as he groped in her clothes. And she remembered being back at school and searching out books in the library when she came upon Jordan reading at his very own carrel.

88

"*Tree, how still and strong to me*," she read aloud. And there was Jordan standing in the bedroom doorway. Phyllis blushed and folded the page from view.

"Why don't you show me your poems?" asked Jordan.

"You'd laugh. Or be too critical."

"Try me." Jordan sat on the bed.

"You wouldn't understand them, anyway."

"I'll have you know, Mrs. Henry—"

"Phyllis Whitehead."

"Sorry. Poet Phyllis Whitehead, I'll have you know I studied the whole of English literature from Beowulf to Virginia Woolf."

"And weren't bitten?"

"I avoided the full moon. Aaawwhhooooo," Jordan howled. He stretched fully on the bed.

"Just wait until my book is published, Jordan. You won't make fun of me then."

"I'm with you, baby," said Jordan.

"No, you're not. But you wait and see."

"How was the tea," said Jordan, slowly undressing for bed.

"All right. But your chairman's wife started in again. She can't seem to remember who we are or where we're from. God, Jordan, if that's where I'm heading, I'll turn in my teacup and hostess napkins right now."

"What did she do this time?"

"She started in again, asking me if we're from the South. As if she hasn't asked me that a hundred times already. I wanted to say, 'but darling, not all Negroes picked cotton.' That's what I wanted to say."

"I hope you didn't."

"I was a good girl, Jordan," Phyllis said laughing.

"But I am from the South."

"I know, dear, and so does she. She forgets, that's all.

89

Then they asked me to join in a poetry reading."

"Your own poems?"

"No, Emily Dickinson's. They're driving to Amherst to sit in her living room."

They both laughed.

"Look, Jordan. We've paid our dues. They're lucky to have us."

"Your father should be proud. We're at Ephram. Aren't we?"

"Don't be silly. He was just more interested in your education and future than your background. Now look at you. A handsome college professor."

"I couldn't have done it without you."

"Don't think you're safe with me," she said as they climbed into bed. Phyllis scampered across the sheets. Jordan caught her by the heel and tickled her toes. His hands moved quickly, and soon Phyllis was covered with him, hands, arms, chest, fingers and hair.

"Well, if you insist," said Phyllis, stiffening under Jordan's weight.

"Must I always insist?"

"Yes." And as Jordan settled her beneath his rocking chest, in the lines of her face she wrote *tree*. The two of them lay rocking back and forth until those lines cracked about her mouth, drew her skin as tight as a drum with the rocking and easing her down and up and as she pushed with her small hips. Jordan's sweat and stray kisses washed the tree lines away from her mouth, but missed the words her fingernails had scrawled on his pumping back.

"Jordan? Are you up?"

"Yes."

"Come back to bed. It's late."

"You go on to sleep, Phyllis. I'm working on my lecture for tomorrow."

"You mean, you can't sleep. Nobody writes a lecture at three in the morning. Take a Valium. They're in the medicine chest."

"I'll be all right."

"Morning class?"

"Yes, and I'm seeing a student in my office."

"Not the one who wanted you to advise the Black Student Union?"

"No."

"Honestly, Jordan. Will those students ever leave you alone?"

"Go back to sleep, baby."

"Don't stay up too late."

Later, Jordan looked in and Phyllis was fast asleep, her head tossed limply to one side, her long hair hanging full, brown cheekbones catching rays of moonlight that beamed into the room. Jordan tried to work again, but his notes blurred together senselessly. He went to the bathroom. Tried to read again. He looked out the front windows and onto the campus green that was thick with night and nothing. He got back into the bed and slept with his arm draped across the small of her back.

Dong Dong Dong
Dong Dong Dong

The brass clasps of Jordan's briefcase glittered in the morning sun as he rushed to the lecture hall. By the last peal of the bell he was mounting the podium, clearing his throat, searching the back wall for his first words, which he found in the faces of five black students, whose too-expectant eyes made his throat go dry.

It was past midnight another sleepless night when Jordan heard voices outside his front window, then footsteps heading towards the center of the campus green. The loud snap of wood cracking in two. By the time Jordan drew back the curtains and opened the window, he could smell the kerosene, hear the crackle and pop of fire. What he saw made his breath like lead. He woke Phyllis and they went outside to get a closer look, to see if it was real. Across the street in the center of the perfectly tended campus green was a burning cross, the size of a man with outstretched arms dressed in flaming rags.

Alarms sounded and sirens screeched from a distance. Students left their dormitories and gathered to watch the cross out of disbelief and fear. The firemen took a good half hour to extinguish the flames, as if to let the burning cross take full effect.

"But this is the North," said Phyllis as she held onto Jordan.

"This can't happen here," said Jordan.

The next morning the president of the college called Jordan to his office. "Not at Ephram," he said. "This can't happen here. You're from the South, Jordan. What does it all mean?"

"I don't know," said Jordan. "But I wish I did."

Suddenly, it was clear to him. He was no longer safe. Perhaps the cross burning was the final revenge of the town. The guilty parties were never caught. The local and Boston papers gave it front page coverage. Interviews with several townspeople were telling. Some said they were proud Americans and wanted to keep their community decent. Others complained about the large number of black students on campus—less than a hundred out of two thousand. The white students started complaining about the way blacks sat together in the dining hall. "Self-segregating," some argued, without questioning their own selection of friends.

But that was just the tip of an iceberg too slippery to hold. A flood of complaints came unleashed: an excellent football player was never allowed on the field during home games; racial slurs appeared among the graffiti of the dormitory restrooms; courses in literature and history rarely mentioned the contributions of blacks; black theater majors were never offered major parts in campus productions. Jordan felt partly guilty and vowed to himself to include more black material in his teaching. He couldn't help but remember his own days at Groton when the film club showed *Birth of a Nation* and how he cringed in his seat, trying to hide. And how he laughed himself silly along with whites as they viewed *Song of the South* and afterwards imitated big-lipped Uncle Remus. And he recalled the dumb wonder of his roommates when he applied Vaseline to his scalp and brushed his short hair to a crisp shine. His thoughts went all the way back to Highway 74 leading into Pee Dee. He remembered his promise never to come back.

Yet Jordan knew his days at Ephram were numbered. One dream kept him on edge. Mother Harriet was laughing at him as she sped the car around the hairpin curve. This time Jordan stood his ground. The car skidded to a halt inches in front of him. The old woman hobbled out of the driver's seat. "So this is why you left?" She laughed and handed him the shotgun. He took it, and knew then what he was afraid to admit: that he could pull the trigger and not flinch, could take aim and fire. But he didn't know whom he would hit, Mother Harriet or himself.

Jordan awoke in a cold sweat. It was only eleven o'clock. Phyllis was sound asleep. Jordan put on his clothes and left for the Purple Pan, the only bar in town.

He ordered a beer on draft and didn't notice the other people around him, the bartender or a loud-talking hulk beside him or the noise and the smoke until the beer came and the bartender splashed some of the head into Jordan's lap. He didn't say anything. Then Jordan noticed the music and the crowded bar. He had a second beer and once again the head splashed into his wet lap.

The loud-talking hulk of a man was grinning next to him. "I was just telling Mac, here. Mac, the bartender. So I tells him how we spooked those gooks in 'Nam. And you know what he called them? You wanna know what he called them gooks?"

"No," said Jordan. "I don't want to know."

"Well, I gonna tell you anyway. Cause once we had to fight 'em up close with bayonets, and I wasn't scared at all. Just pushed the tip in and they popped like yellow balloons. Pop!"

"I don't want to hear this," said Jordan, and tried to turn his head.

"And afterwards, you know. Right when they was still warm, I'd jug them one more time, then run my little finger here along the blade." He licked the tip of his finger.

Jordan felt his stomach turn.

"Killing them gooks was nothing man. They was yellow *niggers* any way. Yellow niggers."

The veteran cackled and hooted and laughed. The bartender joined in. The laughter gathered strength until Jordan was hemmed in.

He threw his beer in the vet's face. The vet pounced on him. "You fuckin' nigger. Fuckin' yellow nigger."

94

And Jordan, without tweed or monogrammed briefcase, jumped back into the vet's face, pounding with nervous fury and hurting with pain. The vet jabbed and punched and both of them fought with more confusion than purpose. Jordan flailed his arms about the beaming, booming hulk, and forgot that he had never learned how to fight. The police came. Jordan told them he was at the college. Not a student. A professor, but he had no wallet, no college I.D.

"You sure, you're not one of them from Albany or Troy, somewhere across the state line?"

"I'm Jordan Henry," he said again. His lips were swollen, his eyes dizzy and blurring. "I teach history at Ephram."

They made him promise not to get drunk enough to fight again. Not in Ephramville. They let him go back home.

Jordan stumbled in and woke Phyllis who fussed about his torn clothes and bruised face. She gave him a hot bath. He ached all over. When his dream came back, he could take aim this time. "You're the one, Gran'Mama," he said in his child's voice. "You're the one."

He fired the shotgun, recocked it and fired again.

Jordan laughed in his sleep, rolled over, and slept long and deep.

Phyllis had a breakfast of pancakes and scrambled eggs ready the next morning. It was like a Sunday brunch. The sun was shining.

"I'm glad you fought that guy," said Phyllis. "But I didn't think you had it in you to fight like that."

Jordan laughed. "I didn't either."

That afternoon the letter reached him. The envelope was ragged at the edges and had survived three or four postal handlings and one scribbled forwarding address to 350 College Heights, Ephramville, Massachusetts.

Dear Jordan,
 Mother Harriet died last night in her sleep.
Please come home. The house belongs to you
now. Remember the house? Remember me? Your
cousin, Jeremiah Willis.

Outside the chapel bell rang.

Jordan froze. They had found him. Jeremiah and Mother Harriet, even dead. And there was no place for him here. The campus green still smelled of kerosene. Mount Greylock was shrouded in fog. The hairpin curve was dangerously alive. And everyone would soon know he lost control and fought.

Phyllis watched him, her eyes tearing, but not from sorrow. Her voice cut him with its anger. "Wait a minute, Mr. Professor, Mr. Reappointment, Mr. Drunken Brawl. I thought you said your grandmother was dead?"

"Well, she is now."

"Don't get smart with me, Jordan. You said she died after she sent you north to go to school. And who is this Jeremiah? Why haven't I met these people?"

"You met Bernice and Hollis."

"But not the rest of them. There's more, right, Jordan?"

"No one, now."

"What have you been hiding from me?"

"Nothing."

"What have you been afraid of?"

"Nothing."

"Well, I feel like a fool, Jordan. All this time your grandmother was alive, poor thing. What will I look like leaning over her coffin, saying, 'Pleased to meet you, er . . . er . . .' "

"Harriet Henry."

"Yes, you did tell me her name. Damn, Jordan who do you think you are? Or I am? I want the whole story."

"You have it, Phyllis. Mother Harriet and I. The only Henrys left. There's nothing more."

"Well, we'll soon find out. Won't we?"

"Yes, we will."

"Don't you condescend to me, Jordan."

"And don't you start lecturing me about family, Miss Beacon Hill. What do you know about outhouses and grits? Nothing, baby. For you it's the Sepia Sisters Sorority and the Jack and Jill club, quiche and croissants. You let me deal with my people the way I want."

"They're my people, too, Jordan."

"Since when?"

"Since I married you!"

Phyllis sat at the kitchen table and cried into her folded arms. Jordan started to leave the room, but stopped. He stroked her hair. He wrapped the strands around his fists, then smoothed them back into place.

"What's happened to us, Jordan?"

"I wish I knew, honey."

Two days later in the early morning, they drove to the nearest airport, in Albany. They would change planes at LaGuardia and be in Charlotte in less than two hours. Jordan secretly wished Jeremiah would not have received their telegram in time to meet the plane. They could always rent a car, drive themselves if they had to.

TWO

Shall We Gather at the River?

1

What had happened so suddenly with Mother Harriet left little choice for Maggie and Jeremiah but to send the children to Aunt Clara's place near Morven until things settled down. Mitch didn't mind the move as long as he could bring along his pet snake. Besides, Aunt Clara had an inside bathroom and hot running water. He'd have his own bed and wouldn't smell Beauford's farts all night. What he didn't like was that Ruthie slept in Aunt Clara's room and they couldn't pass secrets from their dreams anymore. Mitch hadn't told her all about the river and its whisper of welcome.

The day before the children left home Maggie killed a chicken for their dinner. That night and the next Mitch couldn't sleep no matter how many stars he counted.

Mitch had watched Maggie take up the red-speckled hen from the backyard. After stroking its back she held the chicken by its neck and extended her arm straight out. The bird lay still, its wings limp, expectant. Maggie swung her arm down and gripped the neck tight and tighter. Her face was as hard as her fists raising and swinging fast and going round and round and round until only a blur was visible. Beauford's eyes twinkled, his mouth was agape. Ruthie squeezed Mitch's hand as he watched his mother twist the neck faster and faster. He heard the pop and thud of the red-speckled body hitting the ground. Instantly, it jumped up headless and ran in tiny circles unaware that it was dead. Blood splattered on the ground like fingerpaint. The exhausted chicken finally collapsed. Beauford ran to pick it up. Maggie returned to the house with the head and neck dripping from her hands. Her arms had relaxed, and the texture of her skin was smooth again. But Mitch kept staring at her in disbelief.

"Why you looking like that, Mitch? It's the same thing you get in the store. Ruthie, go fetch me that pot of water on the stove."

"Mitch don't know nothing Mama," said Beauford.

Mitch said nothing.

Once Maggie was inside Beauford approached Mitch with the headless chicken, its feathers dirty from the ground and blood from the neck. The chicken's feet were limp and battle-worn.

"Here, you want to touch him. He's still warm."

"Naw," said Mitch.

"Come on. He ain't gonna bother you. He's dead."

"Naw."

"What's the matter, you scared?"

"Naw."

"Aw yes you are. You scared of a little old chicken. You ain't nothing but a sissy no way. Here sissy." Beauford shoved the fat dead chicken into Mitch's face.

"You better get that away from me."

"Come on, sissy. Touch it."

"Get away, Beau."

"Come on, scaredy cat. Touch it, touch it."

Mitch was hot. The dead chicken was waving in his face and Beauford stood grinning above it. Mitch reached near him and felt a loose board. Beauford loomed nearer waving the fat body and poking out his tongue, "Sissy."

"Get away, Beau."

"Sissy, sissy, sissy."

"Get away I say."

"Come on touch it. Touch it."

Mitch gripped the loose board tighter in his small hands.

"Come on, sissy," Beauford started and just as he waved the dead mass to Mitch's face again, Mitch yanked the board up and brought it smack against Beauford's out-stretched arm.

"You God Damn—" The board cracked again. The chicken dropped out of his hand. Mitch ran and kept on running until he was safe in the woods.

Mitch had none of the fried chicken on the short ride to Aunt Clara's. He went to bed hungry. When his dream finally came he found himself running again, not in the woods but up a short hill. When he reached the top he felt water on him. A rank smell of rain. Above him was Beauford with his dick out peeing on him. Mitch threw dirt at him but Beauford kept peeing, and he was laughing, saying, "Yad Yad Yad." Mitch started to run again.

Beauford was close behind with a knife in his hands. He was coming fast. Mitch left the rocks and headed into the woods, running. The ground became steep and steeper. Mountains. Mitch ran until his throat thinned and his stomach ached. But he kept on running through the pines and the cypresses, the willows and oak, through the honeysuckle vines and over pine roots. He jumped between the red graveled gullies and climbed higher. His breath came short and painful, his legs tight and brittle.

He reached a sign that said *Yadkin River* pointing below. But where could he go? Beauford was climbing fast after him. Mitch looked down and saw a star-like pattern of creeks and lakes fingering out of the mountain and what the sign called the Yadkin River. Another sign read *Fork Mountain: Buffalo Creek, Elk Creek, Stony Creek, and Lewis Fork.* The rustling behind him was close. The knife glistened from Beauford's hand. He charged at Mitch. Mitch darted higher into the thick mountain.

"I'll get you Mitch. I'll get you." It was Beauford, not

the mountain breathing aloud this time. But where was Ruthie?

"Ruthie?" said Mitch still running. Somehow his legs felt longer and stronger. Was he moving at all? He could hear Beauford clearer now.

"I'll get you Mitch. Just you wait. I'll get you, you little sissy."

Mitch climbed until his breath was too short to fill his lungs and his throat clogged dry. His head suddenly felt light.

"I'll get you—"

Yad Yad Yad Yad Yad
Yad Yad Yad Yad Yad

Was it the mountain calling him? Was it Ruthie? Mitch's throat was too tight to answer. Trees rustled. Briars tugged at his pants,

Yad Yad Yad Yad Yad
Yad Yad Yad Yad Yad

"I'll get you—"

When the hand touched him Mitch was awake under the sun. His head felt too heavy to lift and his neck sleepy and weak.

The dream shook him badly enough for Mitch to want to go back home to tell Maggie. The house was just two country miles away, and if he cut through the woods it wouldn't take him long. Beauford knew the way back. They'd only stay a few minutes. Mitch trusted Beauford only that far, through the woods and to the house. Then he would tell Maggie and not let Beauford know he was telling.

"I got to see Mama."

"You homesick already? What a sissy."

"I'll go by myself, you don't show me the way."

"And get lost. You know Mama gonna blame me if anything happens to you. Come on."

The two boys started back to their house. They left Ruthie and the two beds, the inside bathroom, the hot running water. The path through the woods was uneven and rocky. Stones and low hanging bushes made Beauford stumble as he pushed ahead of Mitch and far into the woods Mitch did not yet know. The sun sliced through the branches and the brush angry that anyone would pass through. Mitch followed closely behind.

"You sure this is the way?"

"You wanted to see Mama right?"

"Yeah, Beau but I can hardly see you."

"It ain't that far."

"Is that Mother Harriet's hill above them pines?"

"I guess so."

"What's that smoke Beau. I bet it's Mama cooking."

"Naw, we ain't that close."

"Maybe it's in the woods then."

"Could be."

"Hold on. You're walking too fast."

"You just gotta keep up that's all. You wanted me to show you the way, right? So keep up."

"That smoke is getting closer. You think it's a fire?"

"Could be."

"Hey! That branch hit me right in the eye."

"Slow poke."

The sun streaked into the brush where the smoke was

curling up. Beauford pushed ahead. The smoke almost caught them in its trickling path upwards from a clearing, and when Beauford and Mitch pushed through there was the campfire and the hunched back of a man.

"Huh!" Mitch gasped. The man turned around. The lines on his face led to a bristly new beard. The fat scar across his cheek made even Beauford step back. All eyes held for a moment. Legs rooted to the spot, to the sunlight, to the smoke curling up and vanishing. Mitch pushed into Beauford who fell further into the light. The man got up quickly, his eyes flashing."

"Let's get outta here, Mitch."

"I'm coming."

Their legs caught the fire of their fear and the boys were off running into the pines and the hill, leaving the cut man and the hissing smoke. Beauford didn't stop through the remaining brush until he saw Maggie at the back porch sorting clothes. "Mama, Mama!" He was so out of breath he couldn't talk.

"Beauford!" said Maggie, "what you doing here? Where Mitch and Ruthie? What you doing here? I thought I told you—"

"It was Mitch that made me, Mama. He wanted to come. And if I didn't show him the way he'd come anyhow."

"Where Mitch?"

"He coming."

Beauford followed his mother to two black pots cooking in the yard. Soapy water percolated in one pot, the other was filled with rinsing spring water. Maggie stirred shorts and t-shirts in the pots with a stick as flat as an oar. On a table fat coils of wrung clothes waited to be unfurled. It was ten o'clock and drying time. The sun was ready.

Mitch, scratched from the brush and breathless, stumbled into the yard. "Mama, we saw a man," he said.

"A big old man sitting in the woods," said Beauford.

"And he was coming after us," added Mitch.

"You had no business being there no way," Maggie said. She handed the coiled clothes to Beauford.

"We was coming here, huh, Beau?"

Beauford was quiet.

"You must have Aunt Clara worrying to death."

"I wanted to see you Mama and tell you, but that man in the woods scared us when he started coming after us to kill us or take us away. I got scared and ran, too. Huh, Beau?"

Beauford was silent.

"And he looked mean, Mama. He had a line on his face and looked like he was going to grab us, and Beau, he kept pushing ahead and running so fast I couldn't keep up and I was scared but we got out of there." Mitch sat on the back porch, exhausted, his breath short, his legs still shaking.

"Sure it wasn't Lou out hunting, Mitch?"

"Naw, it weren't Lou, it weren't nobody we know. It was a big man, Mama, with hair all on his face like he been lost for a long time, huh, Beau?"

Beauford handed the clothespins to Maggie.

"You don't believe me Mama ask Beau."

Beauford said nothing.

"You was scared too."

Beauford said nothing, a silence as menacing as the piss-stained hillside.

"He had a line on his face and he was coming after us to grab us and eat us and kill us and—"

"That's enough Mitch. You know you to be good at Clara's. Why don't you stop all this foolishness."

"But it was Mama," said Beauford at last, grinning mysteriously at Mitch. "It was a man we ain't never seen

107

around here. And he did have a line on his face, looked funny, too."

"Just like I said, Mama. He was going to grab us."

"You boys see I got my work to do." Maggie lifted the steaming clothes from the boiling pot and into the rinse pot. The shirts and sheets already hanging were flags waving.

"Everything all right at Clara's?"

"Yes Mama," said Beauford.

"Cept I can't sleep," said Mitch.

"Beauford bothering you again?"

"Naw, Mama. It ain't me."

Mitch looked at Beauford grinning behind the sheets. It scared him. But when he looked closer he saw that Beauford wasn't grinning at all. The sheets were empty and his brother stood stirring the pot. Mitch shook his head; he wasn't sure of anything now, not anything he could tell right off or aloud. "Naw, Mama. He ain't bothering me none. I just get scared sometimes."

"Mama, there really was a man and he looked like he was lost. But we cut out of there fast because he was really coming for us."

"You be careful Mitch. You too, Beauford. You look out for your little brother. No foolishness now, Ruthie, too. You see I got all this work to do."

Beauford saw that the car was missing. "Where's Papa?"

"Gone to Charlotte. To the airport," said Maggie distantly, her voice starting to sink. *The line on the face,* she remembered Mitch saying. *The cut line.*

"What he go to the airport for?"

Maggie moved away from Beauford. "To get Jordan," she said, looking away from the boys and into the woods.

Mitch looked up. "Jordan?"

"Jeremiah went to get Jordan and bring him back." Maggie stirred a new pile of clothes. She was still thinking: *The line. The line on his face.*

Jordan, Mitch thought. The name made him restless. His mother, bending over the wash pot and scrub board, her eyes occasionally fleeting into the woods, made him nervous, too. Beauford stirred the black boiling pots. He grinned as he churned up dirt and suds. Mitch watched Maggie, then Beauford and back to Maggie. "Mama," he asked, "are you all right?"

2

The drive from Pee Dee to Douglass Airport in Charlotte took close to two hours. Jeremiah was there in time to see the plane land precisely at ten thirty-five.

Jordan and Phyllis brought one suitcase and a carry-on flight bag. They expected to stay long enough to settle the business of Mother Harriet's death and Jordan's inheritance, which by his calculations included the house and twenty acres.

Jeremiah and Jordan greeted each other with barely a handshake. Jeremiah said little at first. He wanted to hear from Jordan's lips how much he had changed, if he had changed at all except for what the years and the distance between them could make.

"This is my wife, Phyllis," Jordan said nodding to Jeremiah and to Phyllis. He put his arm around her, and they walked to the waiting Chevrolet. "She's a little tired from the trip."

"Oh, am I?" said Phyllis.

Jordan cut his eyes at her.

"A little tired," she said. Then under her breath. "It wasn't that long a flight, Jordan." And louder, "So you're Jeremiah?"

"Your wife, huh?"

"Yes. I'm married."

"Been married long?"

"Eight years."

"Now ain't that something."

"Yes," said Phyllis. "It's something all right."

The three got into the car and wheeled out of the parking lot. Jordan felt the sun on his face. He tried to find something to say. "How's the land holding up?" he asked.

"We didn't know you was married, Jordan. How do Misses?"

"I'm fine Jeremiah," said Phyllis. "Jordan's told me a little about you."

"No, I haven't."

"I didn't think so," said Jeremiah, turning onto the highway that led into Charlotte.

"And the land," said Jordan. "Should be close to twenty acres, right?"

Jeremiah looked at Phyllis. "He don't say too much about his people. Like he shamed or something."

"He comes out with it," said Phyllis, "when you press him."

"That's right, Misses. You gotta press him."

"Please call me Phyllis."

"Sure. Yeah, Jordan the land's doing right nicely I say. Needs a little tidying up here and there. But doing right nicely."

"That's just fine," said Jordan. He looked at Phyllis. "I want to sell it right away."

"Sell it?"

"Yes Jeremiah, sell all of it. And *leave*." Jordan finished on the note he thought would end his tie with the Jeremiah Willis family as well.

The Chevrolet pulled to a stop on the highway shoulder.

"What's the matter?" Jordan looked at the road nervously. There were only a handful of cars heading towards Charlotte.

"Might be a flat," Jeremiah said. "My car ain't all that used to these city highways, you know. This is a country wagon."

"I didn't feel anything."

"No?"

"I didn't feel anything, Jeremiah."

"You too, Phyllis?"

Phyllis looked up. "No Jeremiah I don't think so." She leaned back in her seat to sleep.

"You never can tell about these here roads."

"I'm telling you *I didn't feel anything*. Let's go, Jeremiah."

"I know," Jeremiah said straight into Jordan's face. Their eyes held a long moment. Jeremiah searched every inch of him.

"I guess I best check it anyhow." Jeremiah got out of the car and walked slowly to the back. He inspected each of the four tires, hot now in the sun baking the road. Jeremiah got back into the car and pulled away. "Humph," he said.

From the airport highway the Chevrolet dashed onto East Independence Boulevard that ran the outskirts of Charlotte and led to the small towns. Once out of Charlotte Jeremiah cut the silence brooding between him and Jordan. "Ain't no selling of that land," he said. "No sir ain't no selling." Jeremiah looked out of the corner of his eye. He grinned and accelerated. The green Chevrolet lurched ahead to the stretching hills.

When they had traveled for close to an hour Phyllis woke up. She wiped her eyes and tossed her hair to the back of her head. "Where are we now?"

"Route 74. City folks call this stretch the Andrew Jackson Highway, but we know it, us folks out this way, as Poke's Highway. Road used to be so bad all you could do was poke along. You remember that, Jordan?" Jeremiah laughed, and he laughed alone. Jordan rested against the window, pretending sleep.

Sounds from the countryside filled the air. The Chevrolet became hot inside. Occasionally the gravel whistled below the car's recapped tires and bounced into a spray of hard dust shooting out from the humming center. Jordan watched the acres of green farmland that stretched for miles.

Birds called from every direction, and Jordan could smell the woodsmoke and cow dung, the horses and pigs, the freshly cut grass. Newly planted trees bent and rustled in the slight breeze as the car lurched and careened on the asphalt tongue of Route 74. Patches of red dirt clung to the roadsides. Jordan could smell the land getting closer to him. His stomach ached, rumbling and weak. The turmoil inside him ran from the nostrils stuffing with new smells to his stomach trying to digest the odors and sights.

Jordan had come on business. Strictly business. Mother Harriet's death and the business of the land: red, sometimes rocky, and rich. But something else inside him made him feel light as his stomach turned with near excitement. He wanted air. He opened the car window, he listened. Junebugs and dragonflies scraped their wings. Mosquitoes buzzed and flies snapped at the windshield.

His skin felt light and invisible but Jordan held himself in. He could hear the trees singing as the car lurched past. He studied the presence of the wind and the road. Was it telling him to leave now just as he arrived? Or telling him to stay just long enough to feel the redness of the earth again, the redness of his own brown skin? Something out of the ground was speaking to him. Jordan was checking it, holding.

But the fear was gone. Just like that, gone. Jordan turned to Phyllis. He wanted to tell her about the silence and the country, not the *Dong Dong Dong* rushing him to class and home and to class again. *Dong Dong Dong.* It was gone. The drumming inside him had gone. The insects were cooling him. The smells of the earth were planting inside him.

But when he saw Phyllis next to Jeremiah and Jeremiah driving without a word, he thought he would let her know he was all right and that they could come back together closer now and perhaps, perhaps—

Dong Dong Dong.

"What's that Jeremiah?"

"We passing the old Rockhill Baptist Church. They call it the Good Shepherd now on account of the new minister and the Church Building Fund, but it's the same stuff."

"But the bells. I hear the bells."

"Must be another funeral."

Jordan felt sweaty and hot. In a moment the church was behind them. The bells drowned in the rush of traffic and the steady hum of the road.

"Just relax, Jordan," said Phyllis. She took his hand. "Just relax now."

"We're almost there," said Jeremiah.

"Sure." Jordan lay back and waited.

Out of the corner of his eye Jeremiah looked at Jordan. He could see how much he had grown. Just like Chloe and Harriet would have wanted, he said to himself. "So you married, huh Jordan?"

Jordan shifted in his seat. "Yes."

"Where your people from, Misses?"

"Phyllis," she said.

"That's right. Phyllis. I forgets."

"That's quite all right. We're from Boston."

"You don't look like you from round here."

"No, I don't think so."

"That's north, huh?"

"Yes, Boston. In Massachusetts."

114

"Boston. Now ain't that something," said Jeremiah.

Phyllis was too much excited with the countryside to pay Jeremiah or even Jordan much attention. She felt the sun on her face and leaned her head back to soak it all up. Her hair dangled behind the seat. "It's so green," she said.

"It's green all right," said Jeremiah. "Weren't no trouble getting that letter, I reckon."

"No," said Jordan. "And mine?"

"No, not at all. Ain't too many us left on the road. None cept me and Lou and Addie left. And then there's Harriet's house sitting up there watching us all. It's empty now."

"Empty?"

"Cept a few personal things what's left. She ain't had much, you know. But we saved it all for you. We knew you was coming."

"Any buses out this way?" said Jordan. "We could have taken the bus."

"No trouble at all, Jordan. We was expecting you."

Jordan leaned back against the window and wondered why. The road ahead lay silent and empty.

Jeremiah turned to Phyllis. "You don't know too much about our country down here seeing how you from the North like you say."

"Massachusetts," Phyllis said again.

"Yeah. That's it."

"It's beautiful. Quite beautiful."

Jordan was uneasy and still trying to relax. It was the church and the bells that started it up again. Just when he was feeling different. New. But he had set it in his mind what he had to do. And he would do it. Sell the land and go back. He shifted in his seat again. The air licked him as the car moved ahead, slower now it seemed to him. Slower.

"Pee Dee and Lilesville once was something," Jeremiah

said. "Ain't that right Jordan?"

Jordan was quiet.

"People around here mostly is poor folks. Farmers. Cept for a few what works in the electric plant or the textile mills. And them what used to do lumber work."

Along the road townships appeared and disappeared just as quickly. The steady flash of signs naming them was becoming monotonous. Jordan couldn't wait to reach Pee Dee. Soon came the *Wadesboro* sign and Jordan felt relieved. After Wadesboro was Lilesville, then Pee Dee not too far from there.

"This here is Anson County," Jeremiah said to Phyllis. "What Wadesboro's in. Most folks works in the textile mill. Ain't too bad for a town. The bus run through, got a few stores. We comes here sometimes to get clothes out the big stores. Here or in Rockingham on the other side."

"The other side of what?"

"Pee Dee River."

Jordan was quiet.

"You have a large family?" said Phyllis.

"Just me, my wife and three kids."

"I'd love to meet her."

"You will. I reckon you will."

Not long after Wadesboro the green Chevrolet pushed toward a sign reading *Lilesville, population 350.*

"Ain't too much in Lilesville," Jeremiah said. "Not since they moved Route 74 two miles out and called it Andrew Jackson. People used to pass through there all the time before the new road. The highway. Ain't much now but a dime store and a gas station. Graveyard, too. We lives out in Pee Dee."

"But your letter was postmarked Lilesville, not Pee Dee," said Phyllis.

"What letter?"

"The one about Harriet," said Jordan breaking his long silence.

"The Post Office is in Lilesville. You know that, Jordan. That's all it is, a dime store, gas station, post office and graveyard. Was once that Pee Dee had its own post office. Once, separate from Lilesville. Now it's all joined up on account of the paper company not doing so good."

Jordan was quiet. He knew the story.

Phyllis sat up. "Tell me. They use trees here for paper, not lumber?"

"Oh, some lumber. But you see there once was a big pulpwood factory. International Paper Company they calls it. But it ain't so big now though. You see them railroad tracks?"

"Yes."

"It were a freight train what pass there and sometime a train with passengers stop there. Now it's only one freight train every two days when it used to be three, four times a day you'd hear that whistle coming through. The freight train take the pulpwood, though they ain't making so much now. Folks hardly find work. Most of them do a little farming like we do. Pee Dee got settled cause people found work at the pulp factory. Train passengers too, what give Pee Dee its place separate from Lilesville. Yep, it used to be the Pee Dee stop on the Seaboard Railway what goes on to Wadesboro, what runs on the Atlanta-Richmond main line."

"So Lilesville and Pee Dee are the same now."

"Yep, but folks still talk of Pee Dee as being different on account of the river and on account of the folks still living there and working at the pulpwood factory. It's the river, the Pee Dee River, what separates Anson County where we at now and Richmond County where Rockingham is."

117

"Oh, I see."

"Yeah, Pee Dee ain't nothing now. Had a schoolhouse but folks living in it now. My kids come way out this way to Wadesboro for they schooling. They learning things I ain't never learned. You a schoolteacher too?"

"No."

"You don't work none?"

"No."

"How many children you got, Jordan?"

Jordan was silent.

"None," said Phyllis.

The green Chevrolet was suddenly quiet inside. Jeremiah veered onto a back road near the gravel pits.

"This area still got something, though," he said. "Between Pee Dee and Lilesville is still the onliest place you can get real white gravel for roofing and driveways and building stuff. My cousin Henry work there in Smith Sand and Gravel Company for years and built his own house out there. Remember that, Jordan?"

Jordan was quiet.

"There always going to be these gravel pits. For a long time. This land is rich, you know. Got high-grade gravel, what they call it, rock ores, too. They say it never going to run out. A man still can find decent work here even if it ain't at the pulpwood factory. Yeah, decent work. My friend Lou, what lives next door and what's retired now, he worked here years. You remember Lou? He kin to you too, Jordan."

"Jordan's tired," Phyllis said. "This homecoming has taken a lot out of him."

"Sure," said Jeremiah. "I know. Maggie sure be glad to see you. You too, Phyllis."

"Thank you."

"We didn't know Jordan got himself married."

"It's all right."

"Maggie?" Jordan said sitting up. "Do you mean Maggie Johnston? Maggie whose brother, I mean who had a brother named—"

"Mason," Jeremiah said. His voice got quiet.

Jordan sat up in his seat.

The green Chevrolet wheeled away from the gravel pits and found the highway again. The river bridge came into view.

"We got peach orchards too," Jeremiah said. "And peach processing plants, huh, Jordan? Boy, I'm telling you, Phyllis, he loved to go there. He used to beg me to take him with me when I was working there. He used to sneak his belly full of them sweat preserves. Ain't that right, Jordan?" Jeremiah was smiling as he drove past the sign for Hardison Bridge. He stopped the car on the opposite side. Below was the muddy river, the thick leafy vines hanging over the water.

"That's Rockingham over the hill yonder. We in Richmond County now. It's the river what separates the two. Want to see the water?"

"No," said Jordan. "Phyllis is tired, Jeremiah. We'd better get to the house, so we can rest."

"Sure."

"Can you fish there?" asked Phyllis.

"Ain't much but carp and catfish. Not much. Every once in a while the water gets polluted cause of the factories up-country and the electric plants and the heavy rain what comes down from the mountains. And then there's millions of dead fish floating down. Jordan knows all about that, huh Jordan?"

"Let's get going."

119

The Chevrolet pulled into the opposite lane and crossed the river bridge again. There the sign read Morrison Bridge.

"It's got two names?" said Phyllis.

"The Hardison side is new. It's named after some government man. This old bridge what goes in the other direction is the Morrison Bridge named after who they called 'good roads governor' Cameron Morrison." Jeremiah laughed. "Jordan knows all about these here roads. The good ones. He and Mason—"

"All right Jeremiah, that's enough."

"I was just going to say how Mason, that's Maggie's brother, Phyllis. Maggie's my wife. How Maggie sure be glad to see you. Mason was Maggie's brother before he got killed. Huh, Jordan?"

"Jeremiah—" Jordan's voice got loud.

"We'll be there soon," Jeremiah said.

The green Chevrolet turned off Highway 74, and where the sign pointed to Highway 145 and Morven and Chesterfield the car sped forward.

Phyllis looked around, "But where's that? Not another road."

"Morven and Chesterfield?"

"That's in South Carolina. This here is Highway 145 what leads to South Carolina. Where Moven and Chesterfield is. They ain't too far neither. The Pee Dee River runs there too. Straight into South Carolina. It starts up there in them Appalachias. They call it the Yadkin River over in Yadkin County. It runs all this way called the Pee Dee. Then it goes on into South Carolina all the way to Georgetown. You know Georgetown?"

"No, I'm from the North remember."

And Phyllis and Jeremiah laughed, together this time.

120

Suddenly the car turned left. The shiny green hood focused on a high hill where on top rested a one-story wood plank house, chalky white and still. Patches of red dirt seemed to measure the house's history in the brown lines creeping up from the clay and brick foundation to the rusted metal roof. The front porch jutted out over the crest of the hill and gave the four-room house an aura of distinction.

The green Chevrolet punched into gear and ascended the incline. As the place where he had been raised came fully into view, Jordan's face contorted. The house was waiting for him.

He remembered the hill and the gullies and woods around it. He remembered that he could count the stars there when he was a boy. He once thought he could lose himself among the polished diamonds of the night tempting him from so high. And he remembered the day and the night he was thirteen and alone surveying the land and the dotted sky, knowing he had to leave the hills, the pine woods and the night; the only home he had.

The green Chevrolet stopped at the back of the house.

"Are we here already?"

"Yes, mam."

"Well, now, ain't that something," Phyllis laughed. She brushed her pantsuit into place and stepped from the car on the driver's side. Jordan stayed within. If she had looked at him she could have seen his face blank, his lips mumbling, "It hasn't changed. It hasn't changed one bit in all these years," and his hands begin to shake. But Phyllis had stepped up onto the back porch and was looking into a window streaked with mud. She cleared the glass with her handkerchief and peered inside. She saw the barest of furniture: a wrought iron bed, a lumpy exposed mattress, a dresser with random carvings on the pinewood sides, an olive trunk resting solidly against the far wall.

She turned to Jeremiah. "I thought you said it was empty."

"Ain't it?"

"There's still some furniture, a bed and—"

"Good. Be just like home won't it?" Jeremiah said.

"Sure." Phyllis chuckled as she imagined herself in kerchief and duster restoring the house to its former rustic beauty. "But Jordan?"

"He back now," said Jeremiah smiling. "Just look at him."

Jordan was out of the car and standing near the porch, but he wouldn't come up on it. Jeremiah's eyes fixed on him.

"Come on Jordan and see what's here," said Phyllis. She moved to the kitchen window and wiped again.

"No, not yet. I need to walk some."

"Suit yourself."

Jordan walked to the crest of the hill and back again. He scanned the weedy farmland. Roots and overgrown ragweed poked everywhere. The neat rows of vegetables and corn he remembered had somehow been torn out as if an army had come through sparing nothing alive. Not even Mother Harriet, Jordan thought.

Jeremiah set the baggage on the porch. "You remember, Jordan, my house is at the foot of the hill off to the right. You know the path, or you can take the road. It's all the same." Jeremiah took the key from the glove compartment and gave it to Jordan. The green Chevrolet wheeled to the crest of the hill and stopped just before descending. "Come around six for dinner."

Phyllis ran to the car, her thoughts coming quick like the odors of red clay and grass and tree. "Jeremiah," she said running, "you have trees here something like the ones

122

we have. In the North. New England. What kind are they?"
Both Jordan and Jeremiah looked puzzled.

"I mean the trees, what are they?" she said again.

"Pine," Jeremiah answered. "A whole lot of pine trees.
You'll see." Jeremiah turned to Jordan. "Maggie sure be
mighty glad to see you again." The Chevrolet dipped down
the hill kicking loose the gravel and red dirt. The silence
settling behind it was thick.

3

The sudden shift of gears at the bottom of the hill roused the crumpled figure from its rest. Two eyes, brown with age, opened and waited. The car and its destination had already registered in the mind. The mouth remained tightly closed. The ears pierced the stillness of the room, then halted at the sound of footsteps coming near. The house pounded empty. The foundation built from brick and stone at each of the four corners made the steps drum hollow. One pair of feet was like a marching army. Jeremiah went in. He stood at the foot of the bed and searched for eyes. The life inside him seemed to vanish.

"He's here."

Jeremiah didn't wait for the answer, which was a part of him now. He cleared his throat. "He's got a girl with him. His wife." Jeremiah left the room. His footsteps hollow and no longer his own.

4

Damn kids, Jake thought. From his place in the woods where a fire was beginning under cans of beans and soup, Jake also heard the car zoom past. He raised himself up. His head felt unsteady. His wrinkled clothes and hair full of grass showed that he had slept in the woods, but didn't know how long. Moments after he heard the car stop below the clearing he thought he could come out and see for himself how everything was.

Addie Miller, hammering a mop against the back porch rail, saw him approach through the haze of dust and floor shavings. By the slow sure way he walked, she knew he was no stranger. Some distant kin perhaps, but not a regular visitor. Except for the seasonal workers at the pulpwood factory Pee Dee had not seen a visitor in years. Addie Miller was not afraid. There was something familiar in his stride. Something she couldn't quite place. Perhaps he was just some far away neighbor she hadn't seen in a long time and whose name and face she had forgotten.

Jake's steps were deliberate, testing the ground.

"Evening," he said.

"Why howdy-do, Mister. We ain't seen you in these parts for some time. New here?"

"Well no, mam. Not exactly."

"Oh?"

"I'm just coming home. I been away for a good long time, and I'm just passing through."

"Your people here?"

"Yes, mam. Just passing through."

"And you say you coming home?"

"Yes, mam."

"Well set right here and relax yourself some. Have some coffee."

"Don't mind if I do."

Jake sat in the porch swing and waited. The coffee came sooner than he expected. He drank slowly, nursing each swallow, afraid to show how really hungry he was.

"Been away long?"

"Yes, mam. Been about fifteen years I reckon."

"Lord Almighty."

"It been a long time."

"But don't worry yourself none. Ain't nothing round here changed much. Course folks been dying and getting born and what not."

"Yes, mam."

"Now you take old Mother Harriet Henry what's older than me about five, six years. That woman's been sick so long, Lord, she deserves her rest, all she been through. You know Harriet Henry, what used to live up on that hill yonder?"

"Don't everybody in these parts?"

"She your people? She kin to you?"

"Sort of."

"Well Preacher Franklin done said the prayers, done give the communion."

Jake smiled into his coffee.

"What you look so excited for? Death ain't no thing to be glad about."

"Sorry, mam."

"Your soul need its rest too."

"Yes, mam." But he was thinking. How much would she tell him? How much did he have to know before he could be sure? He finished his coffee and rocked in the swing. Addie Miller sat in a straw bottom chair beside him and tapped her foot on the floor boards. A long silence passed between them.

"And this here Harriet—"

"*Mother Harriet*. She my friend. Don't be calling her out of her name."

"Sorry, mam."

"Poor woman grieved herself so after her boy run off. Oh, he was a good one I tells you. But must of had some evil in him somewhere, running off like he done."

"Yes, mam. I heard tell when I was living up beyond the road a piece near Morven."

"You know I helped bring that chile into this world. Lord knows it was some awful pain in that night. God awful. I never did see no woman bleed like his Mama done."

"Mother Harriet?" *Just how much would she tell him,* he thought. It was already taking too long.

"No, she weren't his Mama. *She* was poorly thin, Harriet's only chile. The others they died being born. No. Weren't her what was his Mama. Were her daughter, Chloe."

Chloe. Fresh and smooth as a Carolina pecan, she danced inside his mind and, for an instant, simmered him. He called her back from death to touch him. Chloe, he remembered saying the night he held her circling thighs beneath his. Jake and Chloe, he had called into her, stinging her breath with his and both of them exploding. *Chloe* he remembered calling as he sent the brown and copper colored water down his throat, stinging, pushing the bright pecan colored woman out of his drunk mind and his body staggering into the dull night.

"Chloe," he said aloud. A smile stretched from the bearded corners of his face, but his face was tight and it hurt. When he touched the wide scar where she had cut him once, her name became a hard nothing inside him.

127

"Naw mister. Chloe's gone," said Addie. "She died long time ago. Ain't you heard nothing I said. It's my friend Mother Harriet, God help her, what's dying now."

Jake froze.

Dying? Not dead yet? For the first time since he'd been back the edge of fear cut into him, spreading the scar that marked him.

"You mean Harriet ain't dead?" Jake's voice thinned out.

"Dead? Death ain't no thing to be glad about."

"But you said—"

"Chloe. It were her daughter Chloe what's dead. She died long time ago."

Jake stopped the porch swing and stood up to leave. Addie Miller felt his strangeness, the same strangeness that came the night Harriet went running down to her, her eyes emptying, her voice gone. But what was that name? Addie could not think. She studied the man again. She could not remember. Her head began to ache.

"My memory don't serve me so good now like it used to."

"That's all right."

"But you don't look so good."

"I'm all right."

"You hungry? Don't look like you been eating right."

"No, mam. I'm fine."

"That's old folks for you. Always running off at the mouth."

"Yeah."

"Funny though."

"What?"

"I mean funny about Chloe. Harriet too. She always said that before she died she would get that nigger what done in Chloe and left her with that baby. But I reckon Mother Harriet done forgot all about that man Jake, that's it. That's

128

his name. She must have forgot all about him since Jordan started growing into his own. He was a good boy before he run off like he done."

Jake felt empty inside, his blood had all but drained out. He could not find any strength, not even enough to leave. "And Mother Harriet's dying *now*," he said, breaking his own trance.

"Been that way going on least a couple of years. But it's worse now. They say she can go any day."

"And her boy?" Jake watched Addie's dimming eyes.

"Chile ain't nobody but God himself knows where that boy is. But look here, Mister. I got a feeling I seen you before. You looks like a Hampton or a Jones, a Williams, too. Who your people?"

"Just call me an old country peddler you once knew."

"Well, country peddler. I'm sorry my mind don't work so good now. But I knows I know you. You hungry?"

"No, mam. I best be on my way. Much obliged for the coffee."

"Say hello to your people for me. I ain't seen many folks in a good while."

Jake Williams moved off the porch and back into the woods. He stopped in a clearing behind Addie Miller's land and smelled smoke rising from another house not too far away. Jeremiah, he remembered. He looked upwards and saw the hill and Mother Harriet's house standing proudly. So what if Mam'Zilie was a little wrong. He was glad to be back. Old Addie hadn't recognized him. Good thing, too. Maybe he was still safe. Maybe the time was right after all. Jake slipped further into the woods and was solitary and still as a pine.

5

The road to Jeremiah's house that night wrote its length and unevenness on Jordan's face. Phyllis was more refreshed in a maroon skirt and cardigan sweater accenting her wheat complexion.

"Do I look all right, Jordan?"

"Better than I do."

"That's no compliment. I don't look too northern do I? Do you think Maggie will like me?"

"Jeremiah sure did."

"I can't tell a thing about southern customs. They'll probably laugh."

"No, they won't. Careful with these rocks." Jordan walked slower than Phyllis, and she didn't even know where she was going. He reached for her hand, Phyllis flinched away from him.

"Why am I asking you? You've forgotten everything. And everybody."

"Don't start, Phyllis."

"You could have told me more about Jeremiah. How scary he is. I feel silly with these penny loafers on a road like this. Where are my hiking boots?"

"The very ones you wore to Mount Greylock?" Jordan sneered.

"I didn't come all this way for a fight Jordan." Phyllis stopped in the road. Jordan caught up. "What should I say to them? What will we talk about?"

"You'll do all right, Phyllis."

"I should have known, Mr. Keep-it-all-to-yourself-Henry. I just don't want any surprises that's all."

"Neither do I, Phyllis." Jordan held her hand this time.

"And no snakes, please, Jordan. I'll die if I see a snake."

They left the road and entered a dirt path leading to a high front porch. Behind it was a torn screen door, its spotted wire mesh lit by a solitary lightbulb dangling from a cord. "Is *this* the house?" asked Phyllis.

"Shhhhh—"

Mounting the stairs they met the odors of cooking fat, roast chicken, mustard greens, and homemade biscuits. Jordan hestitated at the door Jeremiah opened. Phyllis walked right in.

"Evening," said Jeremiah.

"Evening."

"Smells great," said Phyllis pushing beyond them and into the front room. A door closed to her left. Phyllis startled Maggie who was carrying a bowl with bits of corn meal and milk around the edges.

"I didn't think it was so late," said Maggie.

"Is someone in bed? I hope we're not disturbing anything," said Phyllis.

"Oh no."

"You have a sick child?"

"What you say?" Maggie looked long into Phyllis's face.

Phyllis pointed to the empty bowl and the closed door. "Someone sick inside?"

"Yes. My poorly sick child."

"I'm so sorry."

"You needn't be."

"I'm Phyllis."

"Evening. I'm Maggie, Jeremiah's wife." Maggie looked behind her at the closed door.

"Let me help you."

"We ain't got much of a kitchen."

"It smells great."

131

"Hope you likes it." Maggie led Phyllis to the kitchen; she hadn't seen Jordan yet, but she could wait.

Jordan, meanwhile, settled in the one soft cushioned chair. He mused over the change that had come over Phyllis since their arrival. She was someone new here, someone more alive in the back country of North Carolina than he had known in Boston or in Ephramville. Perhaps it was just the change of climate affecting her that way. But she didn't have to come here, he said to himself; *she didn't have to.* But what was happening to him? He dared not think about it.

Jeremiah pulled a chair next to him. "You all get settled in right?"

"Sure."

"Don't pay no mind to that mattress."

"I didn't notice anything wrong."

"It's just old. Got a lot of lumps in it."

"I think it'll do just fine."

"I know you ain't used to it, Jordan. Stuff out here's a bit different. But then you know that."

"What do you mean?"

"Country living, that's all. If it gets too chilly at night there's extra firewood under the shed. You know, used to be chickens up there."

"All we'll need is some clean linen."

"Maggie give it to you. Quilts too. We got extra quilts. And the sun keeps you warm. We been having lots of good spring sun."

"That's good."

"Not much rain, though. How's it up where you at?"

"Fine. A little cold. But it's spring there, too."

"Now ain't that something. Yes sir, spring sure is here. I'm gonna start working them rows some. Used to be chickens up there."

"Where?"

"On the hill."

Jordan looked confused.

"And she had a mule, too. One mule. Used to be a mule up there, but he died. You remember the mule?"

"No."

"You used to ride him. I taught you how."

"No. I don't remember the mule."

"Well, it's dead now."

"And the chickens—"

"They gone too. They all gone now what used to live up there. Used to be a whole lot of farming that woman did."

Jordan leaned back in his chair. His eyes hurt and he wanted to close them. Perhaps if he could rest a little longer it wouldn't be so bad.

"Smell good don't it?" said Jeremiah.

"Yes."

"We do right good eating down here. You gonna like it."

"Yes."

Then silence. Jordan closed his eyes.

"Maggie!" Jeremiah called and woke Jordan. "Come in here and say howdy to Jordan. You ain't seen him yet."

"How you doing Jordan," Maggie called from the back. "Me and Phyllis is getting acquainted right here in the kitchen." She appeared fully in the doorway and smiled. Jordan sat up straight. She was older than he remembered, and more beautiful. He also saw some of Mason reflected in her face. He wanted to touch her to be sure she was real.

"Good seeing you," she smiled. "But you all have to excuse me so I can finish the cooking. Won't be long." Maggie's exit was as ghostly as her entrance.

"We married long after you left Jordan," said Jeremiah. "And we been living here ever since."

"That's nice. I can see you're happy."

"We have three children."

"Three?"

"Two boys and a girl. My oldest boy he and the girl is staying with our Aunt Clara over near Morven. They been there these few days since this thing with Mother Harriet come up."

Jordan saw the closed door. A light came from underneath.

"That's two, Jeremiah. You said you had three."

"The other one, the smallest is sick. He in the room there."

"Oh, I'm sorry."

"You needn't be."

"But about the house, Jeremiah. And Mother Harriet. I understand that the farm—"

"We can get to that tomorrow, Jordan. Tonight you eat and rest up some. In the morning I'll show you what's left since you been gone. Used to be chickens, you know. And a mule. The mule died."

Phyllis and Maggie entered with a platter of chicken and rice, one bowl of collard greens and another of lima beans. The biscuits came buttered and wrapped in cloth. Jordan hadn't been hungry before but the sight of food made him ravenous. He couldn't wait to eat.

"Phyllis say you a schoolteacher," said Maggie.

"Yes, that's right."

"What grade you teach? High school?"

"College. I teach in a small college."

"That sure is nice. Ain't it, Jeremiah?" Maggie grinned. "Cousin Jordan a schoolteacher. Hot dog!"

"I didn't know you were cousins," said Phyllis.

"Everybody round here is kin to somebody. We call them

all cousins so we don't leave nobody out. Ain't it, Jeremiah?"

"Like all in one family. We looks out for our people."

"That's why we so glad you back, Jordan. Schoolteacher and everything," said Maggie still smiling broadly.

"Jordan teaches history," said Phyllis. "American history."

"Here have more greens, Jordan," said Jeremiah.

"That sure is hard, American history," said Maggie. She passed the bread around. "I never could learn no history with all them dates and things. I was real good in spelling and writing though. I liked to read in them story books too."

"Your children in school?" Jordan bit into the chicken. Juice dripped onto his shirt.

"All of them," said Jeremiah.

"They over in the schools in Wadesboro," said Maggie. "Ruthie say she wants to be a schoolteacher. Mitch, he my youngest—"

"The one who's sick?" Phyllis leaned in.

"Yeah. That's the one. I get them all mixed up. They close enough in age. Mitch, he too young to know what he want to be. Beauford, he the first one, all he wants to do is work around the house here."

"He works hard too," said Jeremiah.

"Yes he do."

"That's some group you have there," said Phyllis.

"They keeps me going all right."

"She used to have chickens."

"Who you talking about, Jeremiah?" Maggie turned to Jordan. "He gets far off like that sometimes since this thing with Mother Harriet, and the children gone."

"She had a lot of chickens?" asked Phyllis.

"Right up there on that hill."

"And a mule, right?" said Jordan.

"You remember that mule?"

Jordan laughed out loud and soon everyone was laughing, even laughing at nothing but watching each other laughing and eating and laughing. Then right in the middle of their laughing came a moan. And again, sudden and long. All eyes fixed on the door to the room but no one spoke until Maggie said, "He real sick. Doctor done been here twice. You all have any children?"

"No," said Jordan. He looked at Phyllis.

"Not yet?"

"We've tried, Maggie. But—" Phyllis began.

"We have no children yet and that's all there is to it," said Jordan quickly. Phyllis lowered her eyes away from him.

"You all been married long?"

"Eight years, Maggie," said Phyllis. "But we don't want to rush things. Jordan has his teaching and pretty soon we'll have a house."

"But no children yet?"

"Now their time is coming, Jeremiah." Maggie looked at Phyllis. "Just you wait. You all is still young. Pretty, too."

Jordan spoke up. "Yes like you said Maggie. We're still young." He stared into Phyllis's plate opposite him. Phyllis broke her silence with nervous laughter.

"It isn't just *me*," she smiled suspiciously.

"But I'm telling you, Phyllis," Maggie began. "When that magic moment comes—I still think it's magic—when it happens inside you, you gonna know it. The Lord sends this burning line straight from your thighs up into your heart and back down deep in your belly. The heat just covers you all up, makes you feel good, and you know as well as the Lord do himself that there's life inside you, honey." Maggie's face glowed, her skin glistened.

"But chile," she continued. "You gots to relax. Let the Lord do his work. Otherwise you can miss the chance. I still thinks it's magic no matter how old I gets."

"That's right," Jeremiah laughed. "Real black magic." Jordan laughed too, nervously and from a distance.

"Lord knows, Phyllis, when I had my first boychile, Beauford, what's out to Clara's now, girl, you couldn't tell me a thing. Naw, sir. That rascal jumped through me that night, honey, I knew I was closest to God as I'm ever gonna get before I die."

"Yep," Jeremiah said. "Your time gonna come. He moves in mysterious ways."

Jordan's hunger had passed and his plate was near empty. He ate slower now, placing each morsel delicately on the tongue and slowly massaging it back into the throat. All the while his eyes caressed Phyllis.

Before leaving, Jordan and Phyllis got quilts, sheets, and two pillows. With the bedding held high above the dirt and gravel they climbed arm in arm up the path through the woods.

Halfway up the hill Phyllis tired. When they reached a clearing she sat down and pulled Jordan next to her. The moon was high and here they could see the land spreading wide around them, encased in twilight and thickening into night. And they could hear night settle on the woods. The birds were quiet, the dragonflies gone. Phyllis rested her head on Jordan. "Isn't it beautiful? Just look at that sky and tell me it isn't heaven."

Jordan leaned back. "It isn't heaven," he whispered.

"Oh you." Phyllis pushed him away. Jordan laughed. He grabbed where he knew she was ticklish.

"Got you."

Phyllis roared. Jordan's hands traveled to her thighs. He held her close. His free arm snaked around her neck and pressed her head to his. His mouth searched hers. They kissed briefly. At once Phyllis seemed distant. Just when he needed her. Jordan's stomach fluttered, then sank down. He looked around him at the night, thick now and chilly.

"You hear that?"

"What, Jordan?" Phyllis studied the sky.

"Over there, hear it?"

She sat up. "What is it?"

"The river. Listen."

"You can hear it all the way up here?"

"Sure. Try it."

Phyllis sat still and waited.

"Yes. But it sounds so fast and rough. Is that the same river we passed?"

"The Pee Dee. I'd like to see it again."

"I thought you didn't want to. You were so upset."

"I'm sorry about that."

"Nevermind. It is beautiful, Jordan."

"So are you. I've never seen you like this." Jordan reached for her. Phyllis got up.

"Oh no you don't. You're not going to take Maggie's advice here. Uh uh, smarty." Phyllis moved away. She brushed her clothes into place. "How did Jeremiah say it?" Her voice deepened. *"Yo time gonna come."* Phyllis laughed. And Jordan laughed too.

"I didn't think coming south would be so easy, Jordan."

"It isn't easy."

"Not for you maybe. I feel different here. And I like what I feel."

"Give it time, Phyllis."

"Well, I like Maggie and strange old Jeremiah. What's

138

the chip on his shoulder? Was he always like that?"

"I don't remember."

"You're just as much a northerner as I am, aren't you?"

"I hope so," said Jordan.

"But you have all this," said Phyllis, pointing in all directions. "I don't."

"You want it?"

"I don't know."

"That's how I feel, honey."

"Do I really have to use the outhouse?"

"I'm afraid so, Phyllis. It's not too cold."

"You'll come with me, won't you. Just to stand guard outside?"

Jordan laughed.

The moon grinned and watched them.

Behind them a bush rustled. Something moved on the ground.

"What's that?" said Phyllis.

"Don't you know?"

"Not another river. It couldn't have moved."

"The boogey man."

"Jordan don't be silly."

"The black boogey man *fo'm down souff.*"

"Jordan stop. I'm getting cold."

"Bears ten feet tall, fat scaly snakes. Lions! It's midnight and they're hungry. *Hungry!*" He bent his fingers into claws, widened his eyes. He came toward her.

"I'm going," Phyllis said and ran ahead in the path she saw circling up and out of the clearing. Jordan followed.

"I'll get you," he said running.

"Got to catch me first." And she was gone through the woods and up to where the white planked house was watching and waiting.

The bush rustled again and twigs crushed on the ground

139

until something dark and shadowy like a load on the night's back pushed forward into the clearing. He felt the moon-light and searched around him hungrily. He needed to rest. He fell to the ground and lay there feeling the moon and the mosquitoes on his face. His beard itched. He pressed his face to the grass and scratched. Slowly his hands stretched out, his fingers touched the ground and felt the warm impression of the two bodies that had been there. Jake was not alone.

He sat straight up and looked. The hunger made his stomach growl out loud. He took a wad of tobacco from his coat and chewed it slowly like meat. His chest ached. And feet. He parted the laces of his shoes and took them off. He rubbed the scars and blisters forming between the toes and around the heel. He picked at the yellow nails and corns. The moon chilled him. He needed to sleep. He laid the shoes sideways under his head and stared at the night. The stars shining above were the only sign that the sky was distinguishable from the thick black hills of night. The moon lit his face and showed how hard it was. Flies gathered at his head, but Jake Williams had grown accustomed to their company. The mosquitoes cried into the night around him, sending their whine through the thick woody air until sleep came, and for an instant Jake forgot where he was.

More mosquitoes and flies flew from the clearing and into the treetops. They arched up the hill and circled the white plank house until some caught in the back screen door. Inside lay Jordan and Phyllis. Between the creaking mattress and night's singing insects, the only other noise was the steady pulse-like breathing from Jordan's side of the bed. But neither Jordan nor Phyllis was asleep.

Jordan's arm rested at her neck. He tried to embrace her. But she was farther away from him. He rolled to his side and looked. The long trip had taken its toll in the bulges under Phyllis's eyes. But she was too tired to sleep. Neither could she find the strength to talk. She lay like stone.

Still he found her beautiful. Moonlight from the back window christened her face. Jordan moved closer to touch and absorb her midnight beauty into his solidly eternal day which gave him so little rest. How he needed to sleep. How he needed her. His hands outlined her body almost naked beside his. He could feel her softness and he was ready to enjoy it.

Just when he moved to kiss her, to press himself firmly into her moonglow, she rolled onto her side and exhaled. In an instant his desire disappeared. He struggled to regain it. Her back to him, he called into the forest of her hair.

"Phyllis."

She moved away.

"Phyllis," he said again.

"Not here Jordan. Please not here." She tightened.

"Why?"

"Because, well, I can't say."

"Tell me, Phyllis."

She looked at him. "I'm afraid, Jordan. I know it now."

"But not of me. I'm your husband."

"It's just that. You. You and this house. It's creepy." She turned away and hid in the pillow.

"Phyllis."

"I want to sleep but I can't. Each time something comes to wake me."

"Did you bring the pills."

"The sleeping pills?"

"Yes."

"Jordan don't be angry."

"I'm not."

"Should I take one now?"

"It'll help you relax."

"You, too?"

"Later, I think."

Phyllis found the pills in her suitcase. She took two and tried to relax. She thought of the woods, the trees, the mosquitoes, the fertilizer smells and started to dream. Jordan curled next to her. "Phyllis," he said and stroked her back turned toward him. The moon continued to play on her bare shoulders, her chest rising evenly, her hips thin and soft.

Phyllis found herself dreaming, but still half awake. She felt far from him. Jordan felt her distance and knew he couldn't reach her even if he tried all night. His skin ached. He wanted her, but not forced and quick like on their wedding night when she pushed him out of her because of the pain and fear. But now her fear was his. He wouldn't dare admit it. He heard the house breathing around him.

"Phyllis?"

"Yes."

"Are you asleep yet?"

"It's hard for me, Jordan."

"But this is our house now."

"You mean that? Are you sure?"

"I'm trying. I'm trying to feel at home. It's different from what I thought."

"Me, too," said Phyllis.

He reached for her shoulder and head and turned her limp body to his. He needed all of it now to help him. Her moonlit brown complexion made a strong contrast to the black night, and he wanted both the contrast and the freedom. He pinned her beneath him and breathed deeply into her. Her legs parted hesitantly and he sank inside. Phyllis remained numb. A coldness swept over her. The tension of their bodies grew tighter than Jordan's stiff skin. But Jordan felt it too. It was as if something in the house forbade it, something inside the walls he felt was watching him and turning away. But Jordan thought if he could hold her tight, press the moonlight and the beauty into him, he and Phyllis would be safe.

Sweat dotted his skin. The heat and his tight wet skin were losing him and he had to get the desire back. He dug for it, held Phyllis closer, trying to squeeze out of her and the dead room that something quick and fresh as a river, the river that was then running out of him.

"Phyllis."

Her numbness answered.

"Phyllis," he said again and felt anger mixing into his need. His eyes were heavy, burning. He was going to cry. He gave up fighting inside her. But he was still trying, *trying* to save them both. "Phyllis," he choked, "I was born here." She groaned and jerked him away, sending him up and out of the bed linen tangled between her legs and her shaking stomach; her head was dizzy, her eyes full and wet.

6

Two days without Jake in New Orleans and already
Mam'Zilie felt different. She kept her teeth out longer and
smoked her pipe. He never did like her pipe. But then she
also remembered the neighborhood children hadn't waited
for her last market day and that she had to eat all the extra
oranges and candy herself. And Turé? *"Ce nègre* didn't
have to sell me that rotten squash *non!"* she grumbled
aloud.

In Jake's absence she cleaned the apartment and threw
away the empty wine and whiskey bottles he had stashed
under the kitchen sink. She put fresh soil around the herb
plants beginning to bloom. And she had time to rearrange
the drawer where she kept cat teeth, rabbit feet, chicken
feathers, and bottles of snake oil dyed various colors. Jake
never liked her fooling inside that drawer and always
avoided it, even when she needed something to make
charms and love dust for waiting customers. But during
the night of the third day that Jake was gone, her dream
came back and made Mam'Zilie miserable.

She got up early and for breakfast dipped Red Apple
snuff. She fixed her earrings and powdered her face. She
put on a new kerchief. Her teeth were soaking, but where
were they? She looked first in the kitchen and found the
Mississippi arrowhead plant slumped over. Its jar of riverwater had dried empty. Her avocado seeds had burst open
without roots or stems. She put more water on the river
plant and threw out the avocado seeds. She checked the
top of the regrigerator. No, her teeth weren't there. The
sink? Not there either. Her mouth, fallen and wrinkled,

began to itch from the snuff.

She went to the bathroom and spat. *"Li-là?* Where they at?" she said aloud. She pushed aside the bottles of medicine and perfume but found no teeth. She marched into the living room and sat angrily in Jake's cushioned chair. *Jake,* she thought. She could hear the neighbor's children on their way to school. The seat felt hard and uncomfortable. Her mouth folded into her head; her lips disappeared. Mam'Zilie's whole face seemed to fall as she sat there thinking, listening and trying to remember what it was that shook her so and made her fourth day without Jake impossible to begin.

"Them durn teeth," she said. Then she thought of the head turning in the river. The dream was coming back. She saw the head severed and bobbing in the river running fast and muddy between two bridges and mountain rocks. She'd seen that head before. Head. Then bed. It rhymed. The bed in the window and the house on the hill. Empty. The head turning empty. The house empty. Now the head was grinning with bright new teeth and running with the river. *Running.* The river ran faster through the pines and in it the head was turning over and over, its mouth open, the teeth separating and calling "Zilie, Zilie!" and the eyes fixing straight into her. When she saw the scar on the turning head and the neck cut ragged and bleeding into the river, she knew who it was calling her and choking in the water.

She sat up with a start. Jake and the river! But it couldn't be the Mississippi running right there through New Orleans. Then where was it? Somewhere near Jake. Mam'Zilie searched for the Trailways bus schedule among the papers Jake left by the telephone. She had to find him. Wasn't he calling her? *Calling and turning and calling* through the river's blood? She felt sick and spat out the

145

remaining snuff. She had to get him back before something horrible happened. "Get him back," she told herself.

The chair was hurting her bottom. She shifted her weight but the hard round pain continued. "What in the world—*Comment?*" She got up and looked. Underneath her wide skirt were the teeth stuck in the chair cushion. "How they get there?" Then she remembered taking them out by the same window the night before.

Jake, she thought again and went quickly into the kitchen. She grabbed handfuls of cat teeth, patches of wolf fur, and three bottles of snake soil. She found her powders in a cabinet and took some. In the bedroom she found one of Jake's socks and his comb with hair still threading the teeth. She packed them with the rest in an old suitcase. She'd need everything she could take. She slid her teeth into place. Her bracelets jangled. In fifteen minutes she was packed and out of the door. She went quickly down the stairs and knocked at Joetta's door. Music blared so loud from the radio that Mam'Zilie had to rap five times. When the door opened Joetta was in braids and a torn housecoat. Mam'Zilie pushed her aside and went right in. "Joetta, you coming with me. *Viens vite! vite!* We got work to do."

Joetta wiped the sleep from her eyes. "Huh?"

"We got work to do."

"I just got up, Zilie. I'm still tired."

"You coming with me. *Vite,* I needs you."

"This early in the morning?"

"I'm taking the charms. *J'ai tous qu'il me faut.* We'll see what we can do. We got to work fast before it's too late. Get ready. *Viens vite.*"

"Aw, Zilie."

146

7

The morning fog gave the North Carolina pine woods the thick texture of cotton. A dull disk of sun emanating from the sky slowly melted the fog into dew that settled on the grass and the leafy stiff pines. The dew sparkled from the long swaying silk of tree spider webs and dripped onto the backyard piles of wood chips and kindling. As the sun cleared away the mist, the smell of burning wood rose fully into the air.

The sun followed the two men as they walked through the cornfield behind Mother Harriet's house. Today Jordan would look at the land he now owned and decide what to do.

"There used to be something here," said Jeremiah leading the way. "Something growing all the time. The corn, the chickens—"

"There aren't any more chickens."

"I reckon I knows that."

"It can't come back, Jeremiah, no matter how hard you want it."

"There used to be something here. And I still feel it. Don't you?"

"That was a long time ago. It's gone now."

Jeremiah stretched his arms wide to include the cornfield and the woods, "I reckon it's all yours now. Yours and your children."

"We don't have any children." Jordan moved off to a small bluff overlooking Jeremiah's house below. There were trees everywhere. Scant patches of yellow shining between the green indicated clearings in the woods. Jordan's chest filled with air.

"It sure is something, ain't it?"

"Yes." Jordan caught himself. Jeremiah smiled at him. It would take no trouble, Jordan thought, to divide the land and rent it out, or sell it off. Then he could return north.

Jeremiah came near. "You know Jordan, since you a schoolteacher and all—"

"Not a schoolteacher. A professor."

"Yeah. Pro—fessor. Well, like I was saying, seeing how you a professor, why not get you a job at that little colored school in the next county, only be about twenty minutes from here. Or the one in Charlotte. They gots a Negro college there, they tells me."

"What's that?"

"Oh, I forgets the name, some famous fella I never heard of, or that A & T College."

"Thanks, Jeremiah. But I have my position at Ephram to think about."

"They sure be glad to have you. Why I was just telling Lou, what's my neighbor, you know Lou?"

Jordan looked away from him and watched the sky. The sun warmed him. He walked in small steps feeling the ground.

"You all right, Jordan?"

"Yes."

"I know it ain't easy for you coming back."

"It's all right, Jeremiah, besides we aren't staying long."

"Oh?"

"Any buses come out here?"

"Trailways. At the highway junction where we was."

"Good."

"But they ain't too regular, only between Rockingham and Wadesboro."

148

"Not to Charlotte?"

"I'll take you back. When you ready."

"That will be fine."

"You want to walk some?"

"Sure. I have to see it all don't I? We won't be staying long."

They circled the house again and went down the dirt road that led to Highway 145. Jordan could smell wood burning as the sun baked the kindling piles and the trees.

"That road still leads to the Pee Dee?" Jordan asked. The sun was making the tar too hot to walk on.

"Highway 74?"

"There's a shorter way, isn't there?"

"You remember that?"

"I can't forget it."

"You sure you want to go?"

"Yes."

When they reached the river by the shorter dirt road Jordan's face went blank. The muddy water was high and the ripples coursed towards him. The current was calmer than he remembered. "Let's sit here for a moment," Jordan said.

"We got all the time in the world," said Jeremiah.

How could Jordan forget the river? Or Mason? He and Mason used to fish and swim there, sometimes hunt for the Confederate gold the old folks said was hidden somewhere underneath. The two boys would search the riversoil like pirates or dive under water for the fortune. When it was too cold to swim they would fish for carp and catfish all day long.

Mason was the better fisherman and Jordan the better swimmer. Jordan always said it was his spirit soaring beneath the green brown water that called only the biggest fish to nibble at Mason's bait. Still Mason hooked his line with the fattest worms he and Jordan could find in the marsh grass at night. Mason would drop one in, full and squirming. Jordan would spread his hands over the water and call the fish with words he made up on the spot.

"*Alhooanda*," Jordan shouted. Mason could see schools of fish swim away from him.

"You scaring them, Jordan."

"No I ain't. Hold on. They just scared of that fat nightcrawler you got."

"I should have brought my fake minnows."

"Hold on." Jordan dipped his hands into the water. "*Chigoosay*." The river seemed empty.

"See what I told you."

Jordan bent closer to the water and whispered. "*Matabobooo!*"

"Got him," cried Mason. The carp flapped high in the air and Mason pulled it in.

After fishing the boys would anchor the rowboat in midstream and take one last swim before going home. The day Jordan dove in first and found a metal chest the size of a cardboard shoebox stirred up another adventure.

"Let me see," said Mason grabbing the box.

"Naw, I found it first."

"Well open it then. Let's see."

"Do you think it's the gold? The Confederate money?" Jordan searched the rusted metal box for the clasp.

"It better be. We sure could use some luck. Some money too," said Mason. Their discovery was sure to place Lilesville and Pee Dee on the map, just like when Sherman crossed the Pee Dee River into Fayetteville. Mason imagined what fame would be like.

Jordan wanted to be an emperor. He and Mason could reign over Pee Dee and be rich for a long time. "You can be Toussaint and I could be Henry Christopher," said Jordan.

"Who?"

"Toussaint, you know, the black general in that story Jeremiah told us last night."

"Too—saint? Shoot, why I got to have a name like that?"

"You got a better one?"

Mason's eyes brightened. "Call me Satchmo."

"Satchmo? Nigger, you ain't got no horn."

"Bet you I buy me one soon's I get this here box open. Then I'll show you."

The boys searched for the latch which they hoped would release their dreams. They rowed to the shore, Jordan cradling the rusted metal box in his lap. Mason tied the boat. Jordan searched for a flat rock, found one, raised it blade-wise above his head, and in one swoop brought it crashing into the metal. The latch popped off.

"We gonna look?"

"You go first."

"Naw, man, I broke it open."

"Well if I do finds me some gold," said Mason. "It's all gonna be mine. You can wash floors at my house Tuesdays and Thursdays." He laughed, his teeth like sugar cubes. He tightened his face like a pirate and approached the box, stealthily and sure. His hand reached inside, stopped. The box was empty. Suddenly it was as fragile as a summer's dream.

"Well?"

"Nothing."

"What do you mean nothing?"

"It's just an empty mossy-assed box."

"You lying." Jordan looked for himself. "Yeah."

"Shit."

151

"We gonna throw it back?"

Mason examined the inside again. "You kidding? Just think of what it could hold. We can put stuff in it."

"Like our life savings?"

"Our fishing bait."

"A thousand pennies."

"One hundred Bazooka bubble gums."

"Aren't you gonna eat some first?"

"No."

"Shucks." Jordan frowned.

"Three million ants," said Mason.

"Snails."

"Crabs."

"June bugs."

"Your Gran'Mama's drawers."

"And *your* Daddy's curling comb."

They laughed. Mason had another idea. "Hey let's clean it out, put some stuff in it and bury it for a few years. When we're old we can come back, right to this very spot, you and me, and we'll dig it up and live it all over again."

"O.K."

"But what's it gonna be?"

"I don't know."

"Well think, dummy."

"My Mayor Howard's campaign button," said Jordan.

"My best fishing reel."

"The shiny rock we found the night we got caught in the rain and you got a beating for getting all wet."

"It wasn't funny."

"But you sure were."

"The blue racing car you stole from Barney's store in Rockingham," said Mason.

"The big tooth I got pulled last week."

"One of Jeremiah's shotgun shells."

"A chunk of pickled pig feet."

"Pickled pig feet?"

"Well, you said *treasures*."

"I'll take care of that one," said Mason smacking his lips.

"Did you say *pig feet*? The kind Mother Harriet cooks?"

"Yeah."

"Let's go eat, man. I'm starving."

The boys gathered their fishing gear and the metal treasure chest and left the Pee Dee by way of the Hardison Bridge. The setting sun had turned the road golden. Jordan draped his arm around Mason and they walked up the highway.

Far ahead of him Jordan saw the top of a navy blue Ford. He watched it gleam in the sun and swerve downhill at various speeds. Another big city driver, he thought. What he couldn't see inside the car was a woman laughing and tugging at the pants legs of the man next to her. Her red hair blew out of the car and her cheeks, powdered to a clown whiteness, went in and out when she laughed. Her mouth was a set of orange colored lips curling like bacon in a skillet. The driver laughed with her, his free arm hugging her neck and shoulders, and now and then fondling her breast.

"I de-clare, I de-clare, you does some of the funniest things, I de-clare, I de-clare." The woman's mouth moved as fast as the car.

"Watch me now, honeybunch," the man said as he swerved to the right and then to the left.

"Whoooooo, go on you, Mister. I de-clare," she said. The man's shirt lay unbuttoned at the neck where his white tie knotted loosely into a vee and fluttered in the breeze the car was making. The laughter flew from the car and with the engine the noise was deafening.

The man began to sweat. He served wider to the left

153

and back again to the right, crossing the center lane and rustling the bushes on both sides. His was the only car on the road. The man laughed and the woman laughed and they would not stop laughing not even when they saw the black shapes scatter from the hood or heard the thud against the fender and a dull rustle in the nearby bush. The woman tugged at the sweating pants leg, "Ha ha, go on you Mister, ha ha," and smothered the whine from the Ford's spinning wheels. Five minutes later the driver stopped.

"What's the matter, honey? Why you stop when we was having so much fun? Huh, Mister Hadley?" Her mouth uncurled to a frown.

"I felt something in the road back yonder."

"Well, let's ride back and see, sugar."

The man steered his car into a U-turn and drove slowly over the section of hill he had just descended. The navy blue Ford moved at a snail's pace. On the road ahead the driver saw a broken fishing pole, then a string of fresh fish flapping madly next to a patch of grass. Beside it was a metal chest the size of a shoebox.

"See, it ain't nothing but some de-bris in the road. Come on, sugar." The woman pulled the man closer to her and kissed him. He was sweating. "Come on, sugar," she said again. The driver turned away from the roadside and sped back up the hill.

An hour later Mr. Hadley returned alone. He saw a boy about twelve years old gathering the fish and the broken fishing pole. The man watched him reach for the metal box, close it, then tuck it under his arm as he mumbled to himself. He seemed to be calling someone's name over and over. His lips quivered but no sound came.

That night Jordan did not come home. He stood alone by the highway calling from his empty, shaken stomach and up through his tight hard chest, "Mason! Mason." He tried to remember what had happened.

He remembered the swish of the navy blue Ford and a flash of a red painted lady and white man inside. He remembered that he and Mason had separated to hold fort on opposite sides of the road while pitching rocks at each other, their game until the car whizzed past. Jordan saw nothing but a broken fishing pole and a flapping streak of red on the asphalt.

"Mason," he said. "Mason? Where you go, Mason? Maaaasssssooooon?" He thought he had heard laughter, or was it a scream? He was not sure. But he had to find Mason. Jordan looked everywhere.

The sun was setting in bands of yellow and orange along the steep highway hill. Jordan felt chilly, and he was tired. He gathered up the pole and the flapping fish and the secret metal box. "*The treasure chest,*" he said. But where was Mason? He did not know. He walked in circles and headed near a clump of bushes. Something told him to turn to his side and when he did he saw the bloody head with one eye hanging open and loose and glaring at him. Hot and cold raced through him and he screamed but he could not move. He stood trapped by the blank swollen eye of the head that said nothing, but burned.

Suddenly headlights on him. Jordan could not move. A man whose voice he did not know, "What is it, boy?"

"The treasure chest," he answered. "There was no gold."

"What treasure chest?" The voice seemed kind but strange.

"Mason looked inside. He knows."

"Who, boy?"

"Mason and me, we found it."

"Where's Mason, boy?"

Jordan pointed to the head still watching him. "In the

155

river. I went down and found it." Jordan choked. Tears
fled his eyes. His chest sank to his groin.

"Oh my God, Oh my God," the man kept saying. "I
knew it. I knew something was wrong here. I couldn't
sleep. My God."

Jordan watched the man take a wool blanket from his
navy blue Ford and walk into the grassy place from where
the head looked out.

"Wait in the car," he said. Jordan moved to the navy
blue Ford and leaned against the hood. He would not get in.

The man returned to the car with a body wrapped in
the blanket. He laid it gently on the back seat and got
behind the steering wheel. "Get in," he said again to
Jordan. "I'll take you home."

"Home?"

Jordan showed the man where Mason lived.

Mason's mother and father and sister Maggie were home.
They knew the boys liked to stay out late, especially when
they went to the river, so nobody worried. But Mason was
expected home by nine-thirty.

Before the stranger had time to knock on the door Jordan
had run inside with the ragged fishing pole, three dead
fish, and a rusted metal box clanging against him. The
man with the wool bundle followed. He spoke to Mason's
father and mother who were still as stone.

Jordan sat at the kitchen table and opened and closed
the metal box. He giggled at first and then laughed out
loud. "We found the Confederate gold." He started singing it out, "We found it in the Pee Dee, Pee Dee, Pee Dee.
Mason and me we found it, found it, found it." But everyone was at the back door. Mr. Johnston had to hold his
wife's collapsed head in his arms. And his hands were
tightening behind him.

"You white man. White man, you," the father said

through his clenched teeth. His strength begged to be released. It begged until it burned. The driver explained once again how he had hit Mason as the boy walked along the highway, how he just didn't see him in the fading sunlight, how the boy himself should not have been there. And there was Jordan at the kitchen table, alone singing, "Mason and me we found it, found it, found it, Mason and me." He stopped singing, stopped playing with the metal chest long enough to see the knot of faces tightening above him. "Can I spend the night with Mason?" he asked.

No one heard him.

Mr. Johnston studied the man. He watched each step as the driver returned to his navy blue Ford and sped off. The man's pale features, his car and license number hammered into Mr. Johnston's stone face and stinging fingers.

The next morning Mrs. Johnston found a manila envelope on the front porch. Inside were five hundred dollars in crisp new bills.

At the funeral Jordan held Maggie's hand while sitting beside Mother Harriet. He looked at Mason lying in the pine wood coffin by the pulpit at the Good Shepherd Baptist Church. He thought of the rich treasures they could have found inside the metal box buried in the Pee Dee. The box would have held all the prizes they could gather. But there was only the soft blue cushion that held Mason's head, sewn up and polished bright. Mason looked asleep, just like on those summer mornings when Jordan ran down the hill from Mother Harriet's and burst into Mason's room yelling "Wake up you old cuss," imitating Mr. Johnston as best he could.

That day Mason did not get up. The brown head watched Jordan from behind waxed eyelids. When Jordan saw the undertaker close the coffin he jumped out of his seat and

157

cried, "You can't. You can't take the treasure. You can't. You can't," until he felt his voice squeeze shut. He ran to the coffin but Mother Harriet caught him just as he was reaching in to wake the dead boy. She held him until his knees sank.

When he had quieted down Jordan saw the hole. Mounds of fresh red Carolina clay lay beside it. The box that was wood instead of metal was lowered into it and earth was piled on top. People filed past it whispering and hiding their faces, but Jordan refused to move. He stood guarding the mound until Jeremiah's hand found his shoulder and led him away.

Mr. Johnston had left Pee Dee the day before. No one knew where he was going but Mrs. Johnston did not worry. Her strange smile replaced the crooked line that grief had woven into her. Months later neighbors finally reported that Mr. Johnston had found out where Mr. Hadley lived and late one night killed him and his girlfriend as they parked outside a fancy front door. No one ever saw Mr. Johnston again. Not even Maggie.

Jeremiah rose from where the two men sat. It was getting late and a breeze was starting up from the water. "You ready to head on back?"

"All right," Jordan said. But he was thinking to himself, *I did love him like that.* He walked towards the highway. Ahead of him cars sped in two directions. He turned back. "We'll take the back road," Jordan said. "The dirt one."

And they did, walking silently. Jordan's memory of Mason and his own decision three years later to leave the land where he was born pressed into him as he walked. The memory alone, Jordan thought, can be the painful experience of paying forgotten dues. Jordan did not owe Mason any tears, so he did not cry. But from their friendship he owed him a lifetime and Jordan lived the best way

he knew how. He had been to the water. It was finished.
He could leave and forget it all. He wanted to return to
New England right then, but he had seen something new
in the running river, something new even in the red earth
road leading back to Mother Harriet's. Both were holding
him for unfinished business. In his steady plodding steps,
the bits of gravel punctured him until he felt light.

A fast hand to his shoulder stopped him. Jeremiah looked
wildly about in the bushes, the trees, and the dusty road
itself. The men stood still. Jeremiah had heard something
long before Jordan knew what was coming around the
bend, dragging feet and brushing the ragged clothes against
the brush. Then Jordan saw the man half-crazed with
hunger and fatigue, chewing a wad of tobacco which black-
ened his jaws and made his hairy cheeks appear sunken.
The eyes darted toward him from the dirt and rags. He
looked like the earth itself rumbling under Mason's grave
and perhaps all the dead there in Pee Dee. The man stumbled fully into the open and when his darting eyes found
Jordan's they rolled quickly into drunkenness. The man
lowered his head and staggered.

"Just one of them country drunks from the hills," said
Jeremiah, but he had already seen the face and the line
cutting it.

"How you doing, how you doing, nice day ain't it, nice
day. Pleasing good morning to you both and evening. Good
evening, too."

Jake stopped in front of Jordan. A flicker of recogni-
tion came to him. There was something there on the face,
something there even under the beard, Jordan thought but
said nothing. *Who is he?* In the mind of the man pretending to be drunk and lost and stupid a blurred face emerged.
Jake saw in Jordan's older face what he remembered in
the boy sitting on the oak fence years ago. He saw in Jor-

159

dan's broad mouth the lines that outlined his own under
the dirty beard. And he recognized how Jordan's cheeks
curved inward with the same bone lines as his own. He
saw himself courting the girl who had been his, for they
had loved many times in the meadow above the river which
glittered and streamed below their locked brown bodies.
They loved in the sunshine and tasted its fire. But Jake
also knew he had lost her in the frenzy of a late night cry.
A cry that came long after the day she cut him and made
him bleed, long before the crying too had split him and
the darkness of a secluded room into too many ghostly
shadows, each grabbing mercilessly for the newborn con-
ceived out of love and springtime above the glittering Pee
Dee, but the river was also running and crying into the
night and splitting him. *"Aaaaawwwhhhoooooo,
Aaaaawwwhhhoooooo!"* Jake heard it again inside him and
shivered drunkenly, pretending, so that Jeremiah would not
know it was he, Jake Williams, who was there and who
had lost. He was the one who, leaning against the house,
had let the darkness spill its woodsmoke and fire into him
and the cheap wine burn his mind away moment by moment. And the burning continued long after that night, year
after year, until all that was left inside him, even at this
moment on the lonely river road, were either ashes waiting
to be tossed to hell by the next mountain breeze coming
cross-river and cold, or the seeds of a tree ready for
planting.

Jeremiah was getting nervous.

And Jordan, too, looked into the man's face. He could
smell the dirt but not the wine. He saw the age and the
wrinkles drawn into the man's face. Had he seen that face
before? *Who was he?* Had he seen Mother Harriet and the
shotgun pointing away from him and the newspaper surprise? Had he seen the overalls and smelled the wind and

whiskey covering him then? He tried to think, he tried to remember. His head ached.

"Just a hill country drunk," Jeremiah said again and started walking.

Jordan's own legs felt heavy.

The old man lowered his head and staggered away.

Jordan was nervous and hot and he wanted to leave.

"Come on," said Jeremiah, and they left. The old man staggered towards the river Jordan had just come from. Jeremiah pushed Jordan quickly ahead. *Tell her,* Jeremiah was thinking faster than his feet, *I got to tell her. She'd want to know all of it now she got him, and to get him good like she said she would she had to know, before he tried to get her: "Shit woman, you won't be nowhere around."*

Jordan's head continued to ache. He was tired again and needed sleep. *But the man, the drunk;* he was sure he had seen him before, but where? And who was he then? Suddenly Jordan was afraid. He had to get out of there and out of Pee Dee quick before the rumbling in his head and stomach spilled out. But suddenly he stopped. And he stopped Jeremiah. The other man was nervous, smiling distantly with another meaning. Let the rumbling come, Jordan thought. He had to know, "Who was that man, Jeremiah?"

"We got to get back, Jordan."

"I think I know that man, who was he?"

"A drunk," Jeremiah said. "I think by tomorrow we be through. Yep, tomorrow." Jeremiah hurried ahead of Jordan. And when Jordan looked behind him he saw only the sun slipping under the clouds as if to wait.

8

They had seen him, Jake thought. The two of them and
even the old woman. But since she hadn't recognized him
perhaps he still had a chance. He remembered Addie Miller
who was Harriet's friend and close as kin. Addie also knew
why he'd gone away from Chloe and in the woods. But
since Addie didn't recognize him and only Jeremiah was
there who he knew hated him, perhaps he still had a
chance. They might believe him this time.

Jake left the dirt road by another path that led back to
Harriet's hill. He walked quickly and looked in every direction. "I got to hide," he said to himself. "They done seen
me now. The two of them and her." Then he remembered
the two boys who surprised him in the woods. Maybe they
won't tell, he thought. They too young to know anything
about it.

Through the sun setting behind the pines Jake could see
his shadow shortening as he walked. He left the road
leading to the river and climbed the hill. He crossed the
weedy space that used to be Mother Harriet's cornfield.
It was getting dark and he had to find a place to stay.
Somewhere where they couldn't find him if they came
looking. Somewhere, too, where he could be warm and
think the whole thing through. Maybe he should go back
to New Orleans while he still had a chance. He saw the
grey toolshed in back of Mother Harriet's house where
a light was shining from inside. "Ain't nobody I know,"
Jake said. But wasn't it supposed to be empty, and Harriet dead, or dying? Who could be there? Jake didn't have

the time to find out. He had to hide now that they had seen him.

The door to the toolshed creaked open at his touch. He went in where it was dark and humid. He could smell mildew and old rain. The ground felt soft and the few boards that made a kind of floor to the shed were rotting. Jake closed the door and sat down. He could smell the tools rusting against the walls.

It would have been different, he thought. Different if Harriet was already dead. But why Zilie tell me that? She weren't never wrong before. And me coming out here this long way and them seeing me like this. Like old Addie who ain't had no sense in her head but for grieving after Chloe and Harriet. And that Jeremiah. Him seeing me. Him looking like he could kill me right there he so hateful, so full of spite. And me here alone like this, like I got no right to something in that Henry family. Something. *She was my girl. She cut me for it, too.*

His back relaxed against the rotting wood wall. Jake took from his pocket the green tinted bottle he had bought in Wadesboro and sipped. The water stung him and his back went stiff. It had been a long time since his last drink. Too long. He could smell the dirt on his pants and shoes. He felt hungry and knew he hadn't eaten anything except the tobacco he chewed. But it didn't matter. He took another sip. "Chloe," he said. He touched his face where the scar was fat and smooth and hard. "Chloe." He took another swallow. "That bitch."

Jake could feel the night coming. The shed was cooler. His face ached. "The baby," he said aloud. The boy. Maybe the boy's still around, he thought. I got to find the boy. Then he thought of the river and the road. Jake felt stronger. "If Harriet ain't dead, if Harriet dying, maybe he'll come back. Maybe. And I could tell him before they get me. Tell him so he know what happened himself. Before they get me."

Jake took another swallow and finished the pint bottle. He looked out the door of the toolshed. The hills were quiet, and in the white planked house a soft light was still burning. Maybe he did have a chance.

Meanwhile, during the bus ride from New Orleans to Charlotte, Joetta and Mam'Zilie said little. Once in town they would change buses for the one that ran to Rockingham. It was a long trip, but with Joetta accompanying her, Mam'Zilie didn't mind the distance. She needed the time and the motion to think.

"I should not have let him go like that, *non, pas moin,*" she said to Joetta about to fall asleep beside her.

"Zilie you done said that a hundred times. And I keeps telling you a hundred times it ain't your fault."

"But it is, Joetta, I feels it. *Ça me fait mal. Non?*"

"Hush up now and sleep some. You done wore yourself out worrying. We gonna be riding all night and all tomorrow, too."

"You right Joetta. I'm sure glad you come with me."

"Zilie?"

"Hum?"

"They gots lots of mens out there in Pee Dee? Good looking mens?"

9

When Jeremiah reached his house Addie Miller was
already there with Lou and talking loud. The whole house
looked busy. Lou's shotgun rested on the chair. Maggie
was pouring coffee, nervously.

"I didn't know it then, Maggie. Lord knows I didn't,"
said Addie. "If I had knowed it was him Lord, I wouldn't
said nothing. Not a word."

"But he's back now," said Lou. "What we gonna do."

"Yeah, he's back," Jeremiah said entering the room. The
screen door flapped shut behind him. "He's back and I
seen him, too. There by the road to the Pee Dee."

"The highway?" Lou asked.

"No, the dirt road what runs under the river bridge."

"No wonder nobody seen him till now. He been hiding
long you think?"

"No, I don't reckon."

"How you know, Jeremiah?" said Maggie.

"Cause he scared. He about dropped dead right there
when he seen me and Jordan coming up from the river."

"Jordan?" said Addie. "He seen him too?"

"Yeah, he seen him but I don't think he know who he is."

"Thank goodness," said Addie.

"What we gonna do? I got my gun."

"Wait a second," said Maggie. "We should tell Jordan."

"No," said Jeremiah. "What can he do? It's been hard
enough on him, ain't it?"

"But he should know."

"No he don't, Maggie," said Jeremiah.

"Jeremiah, what's eating you?"

No one answered.

Ruthie came running into the front room from the kitchen with Beauford chasing her.

"Maggie, what the kids doing here again?"

"We came back cause—"

"Out with it, Ruthie."

"Caused we missed it here."

"And we wanted to see you and Mama," said Beauford.

"Where Mitch?"

"Out playing."

"Get him back inside, Beau, quick. It's late enough already."

Maggie looked at Jeremiah. "Why you so mean? Don't be so hard on them. Mitch and Beauford came the first time. And Clara brought them all today. Ruthie been crying."

"That right, Ruthie?"

"I'm sorry, Pappa."

Beauford was moving slowly out the door, but he still hadn't gone. "You better get a move on, boy, and get Mitch back here. I ain't telling you again," said Jeremiah. Beauford slipped out into the dark.

"You think there's trouble?" said Maggie.

"Might be."

"You look nervous."

"Harriet always said she'd get him back, you know that," said Addie. "She didn't know how she was gonna do it but she was gonna get him back for what he done."

"Harriet ain't got nothing to do with this."

"But for Chloe," Addie said. "She told me she do it for Chloe."

"Chloe weren't all that good," said Lou.

"No she weren't. And don't I know it too?" said Addie. "Lord, the night she cut him you'd think it were the Civil

166

War all over again with all that hollering and cussing. She knew he was going to leave her. It's his way. And she cut his face all up for it."

"That's right," said Maggie. "Now I recall it. The boys seen him and said he had a fat line on his face. I was doing my washing and didn't pay it no mind then. But Lord have mercy."

"Harriet always said she'd get him back if it were the last thing she do before she died. It was the only thing what kept her going."

Just then Beauford rushed in.

"Where's Mitch?"

"I couldn't find him, Pappa."

"What you mean you couldn't find him?"

"I looked all over."

"I told you about treating your brother like that!" Jeremiah slapped him so hard Beauford was on the floor and crying uncontrollably.

"Jeremiah!" said Maggie.

"Maggie you take them kids back to Clara's. Let Addie stay here."

"Lou?"

"Yeah."

"You coming with me."

"Where we going?"

"Got your gun ready?"

"Sure."

10

Mitch was in the pine forest running. The sun had long since descended behind the hills and left the trees thick in shadows until darkness covered the woods like cloth. Mitch wasn't afraid. He knew these woods, especially the pines where he and Ruthie played, where she surprised him once and chased him back home. These pines were still his secret place. Not even Ruthie knew all the places where he could hide. Alone with the pines, Mitch was safe. Not like the river, he thought. Beauford would never know where he was. *Never* find him. Mitch was sure of that. Not even Mama, he thought. She too busy anyhow with sickness in the house. Mitch was away from all of them and he wouldn't go back until he felt like doing so, until the pines around him made him ready once again to talk to them, ready to listen.

When he found himself deep in the woods with the soft twilight hanging above, he stopped running. Something twirled in his pocket. He started to walk and felt it twirl again, warm this time and closer to him. As he walked he gathered cockleburs and pine cones dotting the ground. He kept walking. When he found the place he wanted he swept the pine needles into a cushion and sat down. The twirling in his pants kept growing. Mitch felt it lengthening out, curling and stretching to his navel and onto his stomach. "Golly Alfred," he said aloud. "I'm sure glad I found you."

The pine trees listened.

Mitch leaned back on the ground and opened the last

two buttons of his shirt. Twilight on his skin cooled him.
When the snake crawled across the cool space and into
the open, Mitch laughed out loud because it tickled, this
curling and stretching and growing out.

"Yeah, Alfred. They can't bother us here, can they? Naw
sir. They won't even know. Not any of them."

The snake stretched long again and pulled across the
open shirt. It lengthened into the pile of pine needles where
the scaly hide became almost indistinguishable from the
burnt orange ground. The moon sparkled from the scales,
the slit eyes, the flickering tongue.

"Not any of them," Mitch said again and huddled against
the nearest pine. The dream and the river, the mountains
too, came so real to him again that he shivered. He could
feel his stomach tighten, and he wondered if he was going
to be sick from all the running. His throat began to ache
and feel heavy, his tongue thick. But the moon glittering
between the pines made him feel silver and shiny, like
Alfred. His eyes burned and before he could stop himself,
Mitch was crying.

The pines listened and watched.

Mitch didn't know how long he had been there, but it
didn't seem to matter. Alfred had curled himself somewhere deep into the pine needles and the dark. Mitch wasn't
angry. "He's better off here, too," he said, "away from
them."

"Away from who, son?"

Mitch froze.

It was a man's voice. His tears dried instantly. He jumped
up. "Huh?"

The man stepped into the moonlight and stood like one
of the trees.

"Who, son?"

"How you get here?"

"I was walking home. I heard you crying. Are you all right?"

Something smooth and young and different was in the voice. Something that calmed him. But Mitch wanted to be sure.

"Who are you?"

He stepped closer. He stood tall, almost towering, his skin as smooth as the bark of a new tree.

"A friend."

"What kind of friend?"

"Someone who knew these woods, too. A long, long time ago."

"You live here?"

"I used to."

"You don't talk like we do."

"No I don't."

"Where you from?"

"Here."

"But you don't talk like it."

"Can I sit down with you?"

"What for?"

"Just to talk."

"This is my secret place. Well, one of them. I got lots."

"I know."

The certainty in the man's voice calmed him completely.

"Yeah, you can sit down."

"Thanks."

He knelt beside him, and Mitch looked closer into his face. "You don't have any lines on your face. You ain't old."

"No, but it was still a long time ago. I used to come here, too."

"Here?"

"Well, not exactly in this same spot, but somewhere like it."

"Doing what?"

"Nothing much, just being here."

"I came with Alfred cause Beauford—You know Beauford?"

"No."

"Good. Cause Beauford was bothering us. Me and Alfred. Ruthie was coming but I left her back home. They was all bothering us and sending us away cause Mama say she got sickness in the house. You know my Mama?"

"Is her name Maggie?"

"Yeah. Mama."

"Yes, I know her."

"Well we come here to get away from them. They was after us. Even Beauford. He always fighting me."

"But isn't it chilly out here?"

"Yeah. Sometimes."

"Here, take my jacket."

"Thanks. You don't have clothes like we do. Not like my Daddy."

"I know."

"You don't talk like we do neither."

"But do you like me?"

"I don't know yet."

"What's your name?"

"Mitch."

"Mitch? You're not sick? I thought you were sick."

"No, I'm all right. Mama says there sickness in the house."

"That's strange. I thought it was you who was sick."

"Me? No, I ain't sick."

"Then why were you crying?"

"Because, I don't know. I just do sometimes when ain't nobody looking."

"Me, too."

. "You? But you're a grown-up."

"There's no difference, Mitch."

"You sure?"

"Yes."

A long moment passed between them. He stretched closer to Mitch and played his fingers in the pine needles. "My name's Jordan," he said looking into the boy, and then the pines.

"Jordan? I heard that name before. I heard them talking. And you know what they was saying?"

"No, don't tell me."

"Why not?"

"Because I like to be quiet here."

"Me, too. They can't get us here."

"You like the trees, Mitch?"

"Yeah. I found me some cockleburs and pine cones."

"Let's see. Oh, they're big. What are you going to do with them?"

"Paint them. Hang them up in my room."

"Aren't you chilly, Mitch?"

"You already ask me that."

"Funny, isn't it?"

"What?"

"Me."

"No you not. I like you."

"You do?"

"Yeah. You don't talk like we do."

"Is that all?"

"No. It's your name too. I like it. *Jordan.* It sounds big. I want to be somebody big when I grow up."

"Big, like me?"

"Yeah. And with a name like you got, too."

"What's wrong with Mitch?"

"I don't know."

"Keep it. I like it. Mitch, Mitchell. Mitchell Willis. You have a middle name?"

"You gonna laugh."

"Try me."

"Beauford always laughs. He calls me names all the time, too."

"Tell me."

"Stanford."

"Mitchell Stanford Willis. That's great."

"I knew you was gonna laugh. Take your coat back. You gonna call me a sissy, too. Where's Alfred?"

"No wait. Don't go. It's a nice name. An important name. You're going to be big. I can tell."

"Really?"

"Sure."

"Why? I mean you really think so?"

"I think you're a smart young man."

"Beauford say I don't know nothing. Daddy, too."

"And you have a smart name. Real smart."

"Thanks."

For a long time the two sat quiet. The pines listened and watched. Insects buzzed through the treetops. Crickets chirped farther away. Jordan sifted pine needles through his fingers and studied the dark trees against the darker night. Mitch was watching him.

"Why you so quiet. You don't like me?"

"I like you, Mitch."

"Why you so sad looking?"

"I remember you crying."

"That wasn't nothing. It happens a lot. And I can't sleep sometimes. I get these funny dreams."

173

"Does your mother know?"

"Mama? No, I ain't told her yet."

"Why?"

"She wouldn't like it."

"Then tell me about them."

"No."

"Why not?"

"I have to go."

"You sure? Let me take you back."

"It's not far. I know the way."

Mitch returned Jordan's jacket and brushed the pine needles from his clothes. He looked for Alfred. "He's gone now," he said.

"You mean the snake?"

"Yeah. He's gone now."

"Maybe he'll come back."

"No. He's happy here. I found him by the river, the Pee Dee. Beauford took me. His name is Alfred."

"I know."

"He's happy here."

"Sure."

"I have to go now."

"Yes, goodbye."

"You don't talk like we do, Jordan. But I like you."

"Thank you."

"Don't be sad. Not cause I was crying."

"I won't."

"Beauford calls me a sissy and a crybaby. He always fighting me."

"Mitch?"

"Huh."

"Let's be friends."

"All right."

"Come see me again."

174

"Here?"

"No. At the house. Mother Harriet's. You remember her?"

"I still know her."

"What?"

"I really got to go now."

"What did you mean about Mother Harriet?"

"She your Gran'Mama, right?"

"Yes."

"I know. Can I bring Ruthie, too? She my sister."

"Yes, bring Ruthie."

"I'm going now."

"You won't get lost?"

"I know the way back."

"You sure?"

"Goodbye, Jordan."

Jordan listened for the boy's footsteps, but Mitch had slipped away so quietly and so deep into the forest that Jordan hardly knew he was gone except for the pine needles still pressed into the ground where he sat. He felt incomplete. Something was missing. After several minutes Jordan got up to leave. He could feel the pines listening and watching as he walked through the woods and up the hill. Jordan also knew the way back.

11

That morning Phyllis had cleaned the wood stove and the kitchen pots. She was glad to get acquainted with the house in her own time. The country was beginning to re-fresh her in a way she could not explain to Jordan. She had more energy, it seemed. And she was more alive. But as soon as Jordan left with Jeremiah to survey the land, Phyllis opened the suitcase anyway and found the pink writing paper where she had also put her pink sleeping pills. What she had written days ago Jordan could not see. "Not yet," she said to herself. "He'd laugh and I'd feel silly."

But it wasn't silly. She liked trees and gardens, plants, anything with wide hand-size leaves like the maple she remembered applauding dawn and scratching all of Ephram-ville into focus. Dawn in Pee Dee was a hoarse rooster. The days smelled like fertilizer, and everywhere was the threat of snakes. Why did she come south?

Trees, she thought. Jeremiah said there were lots of trees. She knew the maples and the white oaks of New England, but what were these? Cypresses, wide and fingery, willows leaning over the water, elm and oak, pecan trees, honeysuckle vines and creepers stretching along the ground, the hanging tree moss like solid dew dressing the forest, and the pines, short needle pines and long leaf pines, the Christmas evergreens. The trees in Boston she knew from the Fenway she used to cross after classes. The uni-versity had shady maples where she had met Jordan Henry; bright, promising, impatient and awkward, who walked with her in the Boston Commons or spent summers with her eating peanuts and reading by the lake and trees of the Boston Gardens.

Trees. She remembered the man who followed her, who chased her, who touched her and made her feel dirty, who made her scream until people crowded around and the police came, but only after she had fought him off herself and went running in circles of fear. But Jordan didn't know *all* of this. She kept it to herself along with the mystery of her trees. Phyllis found the pink paper folded twice near the bottle of pills. She read:

> Corner seeds and scratch the sky
> Nest a bird and make him fly
> Tree how still and strong to me
> Your root of pain and misery.

It needed something more. Something to finish it off, complete it so she wouldn't have to think about it again. *Tree.* She folded the page and went outside.

That was the morning: cleaning the kitchen, searching through the house, trying to write. In the afternoon she found some smoked ham and cheese in the kitchen cabinet and made herself a sandwich. She was glad to be alone. She sat on the front porch overlooking the hill and trees and rocked where Mother Harriet must have rocked.

The sandwich finished, Phyllis remembered the trunk in the bedroom. Perhaps she could find some of Jordan's old things to take back with her. Antiques. Old family documents. Letters, diaries, deeds, birth certificates, the family Bible? Yes, artifacts, Phyllis was sure, that make families. *And break them,* said another voice within.

She went back to the bedroom and opened the olive trunk. She dug through it, sorting the old clothes, the family pictures. But where were the letters? The diaries? The old jewelry? Phyllis found none of these and the smell from the trunk was clogging her nose. But she did find several pages torn from a church hymnal, a broken fishing pole, a woman's dress two sizes too small for her, and stiff yellow newspapers. "Humph," Phyllis said. She left the trunk open, disarrayed. She went out for air.

The sun was fading and Phyllis felt bored. The slowness of the day matched her feelings about the South: hot, languid, thick with musty odors, slow. Too slow. She fought back inertia. She thought of Maggie and the sick child. Perhaps Maggie needed some help. She did say she had lots of work to do around the house. Some to share maybe. Anything to do. But where is that path? The dirt road is probably better.

Phyllis started downhill and had not gone five feet when something black and scaly wiggled in front of her and hissed at the hard red dirt. Phyllis caught her breath. She shivered. Closed her eyes. Touched her heart. The swish of grass parting on the opposite side of the road told that the snake had gone. She felt cold. She continued walking until she stepped on what felt like dried skin. She looked and found it was a toad flattened into the gravel by somebody's automobile. Then she saw it head on, coiled right in the middle of the road, sunning itself, the scales glistening like jewels. The coal black head watched her. The tongue darted out. Goose pimples inched onto Phyllis's back; she felt colder. Two snakes in one day on one road were just too much. She ran back to the house and slammed the screen door.

Inside, she took out another sheet of paper, pink like the sleeping pills, but she couldn't write. She looked inside the trunk again. She brushed aside the stiff newspapers, the dress, and opened the hymnal. The edges had worn thin and the binding had the flaky green grey color of mildew. The loose pages cracked to her touch as did the hard newspapers. On the first page of the hymnal someone had written "Rockhill Baptist Church," and when she opened the book more brittle pages fell into her lap.

Phyllis read the songs, at first because there was nothing else to do, but the words on one page kept coming back to her and she finally read them aloud:

> Jesus keep me near the cross
> There a precious fountain
> Free to all a healing stream
> Flows from Calvary's mountain.

> In the cross, in the cross
> Be my glory ever
> Till my raptured soul shall find
> Rest beyond the river.

The screen door flapped shut. "I remember that," said Jordan coming into the bedroom. Already it was night. "It goes something like this." He hummed the tune.

"I didn't know you sing."

"I didn't either," said Jordan laughing.

"Try this one, since you're so smart," Phyllis said, pulling another yellowed page from the hymnal. "Someone wrote this one out. There's no music. I can barely read the thing."

"We didn't have too many hymnals at the church," Jordan said sitting next to her. "Most of the people knew the songs by heart. And then if you couldn't remember the tune by ear you wrote the words down as fast as you could before they changed them or added more verses."

"This person certainly was in a hurry, listen."

When you walk-a that lonesome Valley,
You got tuh walk it by yo'self;
No one heah may walk it with you
You got tuh walk it by yo'self.

"Like it?"
"Yes. There's more, too:"

When you reach the rivah Jurdun
You got tuh cross it by yo'self

"Is that Jordan? I mean the river Jordan?"
"Mother Harriet named me."
"It's not a bad name."
"No jokes, Phyllis."
"I mean it. Listen, there's more:"

No one heah may cross it with you
You got tuh cross it by yo'self.

"It's not bad. Kind of poetic. Jurdun, like that. Can I call you Jurdun."
"No."
"Jurdun?" Phyllis looked hard at him. "Jurdun. Ha ha, Jurdun."
Jordan grabbed her waist and tickled. Phyllis roared and pushed him away. He was on her again tickling wildly with Phyllis kicking the trunk and the hymnal pages flying about the room.
"Cut it out, Jordan."
"You started it."
"Help me get these pages back together. I want to keep them."
"What for?"

"Souvenirs."

"They were Mother Harriet's favorites. My mother's too."

"Why don't you ever talk about her."

"I didn't know her, except for what Mother Harriet told me."

"Her name was Chloe?"

"How did you know that?"

"Look." Phyllis showed him the page with the hand-written song. The signature inched along the yellow bottom with empty spaces between each letter, C h l o e. The name stared at him, C h l o e h e n r y.

"Chloe Henry," Jordan read aloud.

"There's poetry in that."

"It's just a regular name in these parts."

"I mean the song, silly, I'm keeping it."

"No."

"Why not."

"I don't think it's right."

"She was your mother."

"It should stay here in the house where she was."

"Chloe?"

"And Mother Harriet."

"There's too much junk in here already."

"It's not junk."

"Jordan, you're too serious. There's nothing here but broken toys and clothes and half a fishing pole."

"A fishing pole?"

"Half of one." Phyllis searched the trunk and pulled out the wooden blue pole with bent metal eye at one end. Yellow and red bands decorated the blue at points along the rod until the bottom came jagged and abrupt.

"Well?" she said.

"It belonged to a friend of mine."

"Who?"

"It's not important."

"Why do you always get so quiet when it comes to things like this?"

"I don't know."

"This is your home, Jordan."

"You don't have to remind me."

"I thought you'd forgotten. But where's the other half?"

"Lost somewhere, I don't know. A highway. A river."

"The river we passed coming here?"

"I thought you would have forgotten about that."

"No, I remember things, Jordan."

"I'm afraid you do."

"Why don't you give me a chance, sometimes?"

"A chance for what? To call me *Jurdun* a hundred times."

"You don't think I'm worth any of it, do you?"

"What, Phyllis?"

"This. All of it. The house. You."

Jordan looked away. Phyllis searched the box again.

"What's this from?" she said and pulled up from the bottom corner a pen knife with an imitation pearl handle. The blade had rusted inside the handle. And when she touched it the orangey red dust came off on her hands.

"Ha, that was a Christmas present." Jordan was laughing distantly. "It doesn't mean a thing."

"Like most of this stuff. Where are your antiques, the lost heirlooms of the Henry family?"

"There never was much."

"And what there is you keep to yourselves. Make a joke about it so nobody else will know. That's selfish."

"What are you talking about?"

"You. This house, too. Why won't you let me share in some of it?"

"There's nothing to share."

"Don't tell me you been moping about this place because of nothing. But that's all right. Stay selfish. You only think about yourself anyway. You and your sad little life here."

"You get away from that trunk."

"What?"

"Get away, I said."

"No."

"Get away, Phyllis." Jordan pushed her back and away from the trunk and slammed it shut, his hands holding the lid flat, his face turned away from her.

"Crazy. Sometimes I think you're crazy, Jordan."

"I am."

"I mean real crazy, Jordan. Mad, crazy, gone."

Jordan was silent. Phyllis could see his shoulders heaving and his fingers trembling over the shut olive trunk.

"Why are you trembling?"

Jordan was silent. She put her arms around his waist, "Jordan, Jordan, it's all right. I'm sorry."

"I didn't mean to be angry like that, Phyllis. It's just that I'm trying to understand it all. And it doesn't make any sense. I feel I'm close to discovering something, but I don't know what it is."

"Tell me."

"I don't know what it is. It's something about me, about who I am. It scares me. It really does."

"I feel close to something too, Jordan. I tried to write it down but nothing would come. It scares me, too. And I'm not even from the South."

"Really?" Jordan turned to face her. "Will you show me some day what you write?"

"Will you try to understand it? No games?"

"Yes."

"There, you have me."

"Do I really?"

"Yes," said Phyllis pressing closer to him.

"But I need you all the way."

"I'm yours."

"You know it's not as easy as that. You hold back from me. Am I that much of a monster?"

"Sometimes you are. It's scary. Even making love. I don't know."

"It doesn't have to be."

"But what about you, Jordan?"

"Sometimes it *is*." Jordan pulled her close to him. "They say you have to be free to enjoy love, and I'm not free. Not yet anyway."

"You think so?"

"But sometimes we just don't want to be free, or loved."

"Do you want that, Jordan?"

"I think so."

"Then take me with you."

"It's a hell, Phyllis."

"I know."

"I'm a walking hell. Everything I touch burns up. Burns inside, too."

"I know," Phyllis looked down at herself.

"From all I've come from, my past, Phyllis. It's a hell."

"It isn't that simple," she said.

"Why?"

"I'm a part of this too, Jordan. Not just you. I'm afraid, too. What is a black girl from Massachusetts doing here? Are these my people? And these trees, God!" Phyllis looked at herself again and searched for the words to tell him more about the time, years ago when she was followed by the strange man as she walked home. It was late afternoon, much later than she had thought, and she was only seventeen. She could not find the words. She could not tell him how she started running when she saw him getting close to her. Or say just how she felt when he caught up to her and stuck his panting face into hers, chilling her inside; that Jordan's passion was like his, strong, awkward, overpowering and desperate. Nor could she say how the man threw her to the cold ground, or that she bit his neck and kicked him in the groin, that people were watching her and not helping, that she kicked hard and ran into the streets and back again and that nightmares repeated the experience for her years after. "Yes," Phyllis said aloud. "My hell, too." She wanted him to know she loved him and if he would just give her the time she needed she would love him freely and completely. Then maybe the Fenway, the tree, the cold, cold ground, the tree and the roots would disappear. Maybe. That's why she was here, with her northern accent, her northern pain.

"We can make it together, can't we?" Jordan asked.

Phyllis looked directly at him. Her eyes were wet. "We still have a chance?"

"Yes, that's why we're here."

"I do love you, Jordan. It's just that one minute I feel I belong here, the next minute I don't. Is that so terrible?"

"No, I love you too. I need you beside me. Especially now."

"Now?"

"For always, but especially now. I can't explain it all yet, but I feel it crawling inside me. It's something that boy said. I saw him on my way back."

"What boy?"

"Mitch. Jeremiah's son."

"He's supposed to be sick."

"I guess Maggie's got the names mixed up again."

"That's odd. But what is this thing, Jordan?"

"I don't know. I just don't know. But are you with me, Phyllis? That's important."

"Yes."

They embraced tightly. Jordan could feel her breath move with his own. They seemed more at one then, standing with head snug against chest, than in all those restless hours in bed. Jordan's chin rested against the top of her head. He caressed her gently. "Let's go to sleep," he whispered. "Without the pills this time."

12

The toolshed was hot. The mosquitoes had found him. Jake watched the back of the house until he made up his mind to talk to whomever was inside. Just as he emerged fully into the open the light in the house went out. His decision moved him. They would have to believe me, he thought. But outside the toolshed the night was a solid black wall. Neither the trees nor the road beside the house were distinguishable. Jake felt the night cover him all over. The fresh air felt good but he was afraid he would fall against something. He held out his hands to feel his way toward the house. His feet dragged cautiously like those of a blind man.

Phyllis heard the noise first, a slow heavy shuffling on the ground. She felt cold and turned her head away from the open window. The field crickets had stopped chirping. Lou's dog that usually howled at distant shadows hushed. No night breezes traveled up from the river. Not a fly or mosquito buzzed. Someone had silenced all of nature.

She felt cold again and snuggled close to Jordan, at the same time shooing away the notion of a nightmare. She tried to think of the trees again: the trees in Boston, the Pee Dee, the river she remembered running fast. The colors, too, and she wrote in her mind, *black red brown I feel your tree, the earth of you I am* and the tree appeared again and from somewhere outside her the word child stood. *Child.* Mitch? The sickness? Her own child someday? Phyllis shivered closer to Jordan. *Tree, child, tree-child,* she mused while Jordan slept, oblivious to the shuffling in the night or the silent rummagings in her mind.

In his sleep Jordan imagined falling slow motion into a soft empty well. He wondered where the water was. His throat felt dry and he tumbled through layers of white linen, searching for water, his lips sucking at the tight air, and falling deeper and deeper down.

The noise came again, louder this time. *Treechild, treechild.* Someone chopping at a tree, Phyllis thought. And a tree falling. *Ffffaaaalllliiiinnnngggg!* The noise was like a chain rattling or dragging across the wooden planks of the back stoop and coming through the window. Jordan shifted his arm; the sound was already a part of his dream. Each time he bumped the hardening sides of the well they clanged like hollow rusty bells. *Dong Dong Dong Dong Dong.*

Shadows passed the window. The tree was crashing down on her. Phyllis twitched away from the sound and felt the presence of someone else. She was cold again and when she looked she thought she saw a face in the darkness. Her eyes opened wider and out of the dark two brighter eyes shone like lights of a distant automobile swerving madly downhill and making the trees bend upon her. Instantly, they registered fear. It was the man again, the man chasing her through the Fenway and the people watching, not helping, and she had to get away. She would not let him get her this time. *Tre Tre Tree, treechild.* Her lips stuttered dry; how could he have followed her here to North Carolina?

"Jordan?" Phyllis said, her voice like sandpaper. "Jordan." Her voice strained into a scream. The eyes were on her and the smells of woodsmoke, tobacco and whiskey were choking her. The face sweating on her was real. "Jordan, there's a man in here."

A hand upon her tried to hold her mouth still, to keep her quiet while another hand fumbled at her throat. She kicked and kicked hitting Jordan and the smelly body next to her until Jordan was awake in an instant and bounding from the bed. He caught the intruder from behind the meaty neck where sweat was running fast. He threw the man off and Phyllis saw from the window light a glint of steel.

"He's got a knife," she cried. She kicked herself fully loose and Jordan threw the man against the opposite wall. His only advantage was gone. He had caught the intruder from behind but now he faced him head on. Both men's sweating faces gleamed in the moonlight. Jordan felt the smell and the dirt coming at him. He remembered the odor of wine, urine, woodsmoke, and dirt. And the smell was clawing him with black hardened hands squeezing his neck. Jordan struggled his arms loose and clapped the man's ears. The man released him but found a foot in his groin and then before he could turn away a fist square in his jaw where the teeth and bones cracked under the weight.

But the man swung back and knocked into Jordan's tight empty stomach. Jordan rolled over and hit the floor; the man's fists were on his back and then the hands reaching for the throat again. The knife glinted from the man's back pocket. He drew it out. The point gleamed. Time didn't give Jordan a chance to ask why but he realized that the man did not want his wife, he wanted *him*. The darkness, the sweating odor, the knife told him he'd better fight for his life.

Phyllis shivered in an opposite corner. Her tears made her face icy. "Run for help. Get Jeremiah!" Jordan yelled to her and wrestled the man into the corner she fled from. The knife glinted between them and the sweating stench of caged animals.

In no time Phyllis was out of the house and running. The darkness dazed her. She couldn't find the path or the

189

road. She kept running. She had to come to the road sometime. The trees pressed into her and the bushes cut her nightclothes. Rocks cut her feet but she ran and ran until she felt her chest come straight up into her throat and her breath stop. But she ran and kept on running. She pounded her insides out. She fell onto the road skinning her face. She got up running again until she reached the bare lightbulb gleaming from Jeremiah's back porch as if from a lighthouse. She raced into the front room. There was Addie fast asleep over a plate of chicken and rice. The lights were on but there was no one else. Phyllis looked quickly. The door to the back bedroom was open. *Maggie*, Phyllis thought, *the sick child.* She ran into the room, "Maggie, Maggie!" Phyllis saw it on the bed but she didn't know what it was. Something crumpled into a ball: a round grey something poking from a mountain patchwork of quilts. Something brown, something grey and hairy.

Then it moved.

Phyllis's hand locked in her mouth. Her teeth worked on it. Her eyes held. The mound rolled towards her. But Phyllis remained mute as stone. The mound faced her. The two eyes that had already seen a lifetime stood out from the wrinkled brown head and drilled her. Phyllis felt the edges of knives upon her. But the eyes kept looking into her, seeing perhaps what the man and the trees had seen.

"You. You."

Phyllis said nothing. She heard the voice of a woman. A woman older than Phyllis could ever imagine.

"You his wife."

Phyllis was speechless. She felt the size of an ant running blindly beneath a weight that could crush her in an instant. Phyllis could not find her own body. She had no voice.

"You his wife. He come back to me. You. You his wife."

Phyllis looked at herself and saw the scratched feet, the torn nightclothes, the legs bruised and bleeding. Her joints ached from the running but she could not speak *because the man's hot breath was on her again.* She talked fast to keep him away, "Yes. Yes."

"You mine, too, huh?" Mother Harriet said staring at her.

"Yes." *His smell from the dirt on his face reached out for hers.* She stepped back.

"Is you afraid?"

"Yes." Phyllis was trembling cold *but she told the man again to please leave her alone. She was only seventeen.*

"Don't be, my chile. He needs you now and so does I. I needs you, too."

"I, I don't understand. I can't help. I can't."

"You can if you believes."

"No!" *She pushed the sweating face away from her and bit the neck.*

"If you wants to believe," Mother Harriet said again.

"What can I do? Nothing. Nothing." The trembling stopped when Phyllis started to cry. She was exhausted and tears ran quickly over her face *like the fear that had made her legs kick and dance wildly until she found the man's groin.*

"If you wants to believe. You his wife. You my chile, too," Mother Harriet continued softly, her voice soothing. "I had me a chile once, a daughter. Jordan's Mama. She died birthing so I kept him. Me. But I always knew Jordan was a gift coming like that. Even killing Chloe like it done. He was my gift and now he yours. You got to love him in spite of himself. You got to know that. If you wants to love and be my chile too. You his wife. He left here once, long time ago. But he back now. Yeah, he come back and that makes all the difference in the world." Her voice was calm. Mother Harriet's lips cracked and bled as she talked.

Phyllis stood listening. *"Aaggh!" the man yelled at her again. His spit dripped from the shaking lips.*

"He done come back," said Mother Harriet, but more to herself than to Phyllis trying to balance her shock and put the man, the house, and treechild out of her skin. Completely. *The face, the cold frosty face breathing down into her—the man, the man. "Noooooo," she yelled back and sweat rained from the forest of her hair.* She stuttered aloud this time and gave her stomach a rest from the tangled words "th-th-the f-f-f-face. Him. Yes, a man came in. . . . He came into the house . . . your house. He tried to kill me. . . . We need help right away. We need help. An old man. It was an old smelly man that came in and tried to kill me." She was panting again and wanted to cry. "The smells of woods. Urine . . . and a knife. . . . He had a knife. He'll kill Jordan!" Phyllis went to the old woman's side. She buried her face into the bones wrapped in patchwork, medicine, and dry blood. She cried into all of it.

"Look at me. You listen now."

Phyllis looked into the eyes.

"It his Daddy."

"His what?"

"Daddy. It his Daddy, what come back, too. But we ready for him, now."

"But it can't be. Jordan said his father died years ago."

"Believe me. It his Daddy, what's called Jake. And Jordan gonna know it when it time for him to know."

"But when?"

"After it done. Ain't nothing to stop it now."

"What are you talking about? My husband's probably dying right now."

192

Mother Harriet's eyes rolled weakly to the back of her head. "Yes, he have to die." Her voice drifted away.

"No!" Phyllis jumped from the bed and was at the door.

"Wait," Mother Harriet called.

"No I can't. I have to be with him. Where's Jeremiah, where's Maggie? Jordan needs me!" Phyllis ran from the room, her nightclothes tearing after her.

The old woman continued mumbling, her voice drifting farther and farther away. "You can't help him. He got to do it. It's him what got to do it all. That old nigger got to die so I can die. Ain't that right, Chloe? Where's my baby Chloe? *Jordan,* yes it's Jordan, I can rest so Jordan can live, Jordan now that he come back. . . ." Her voice trailed into itself like water, her head swinging slowly back to a mound: "Yes. We the surprise now."

Their two bodies were shadows that cut and bumped and sliced and groaned their anger into a frenzy of red watered by sweat and spit from both of them. Blood spattered on the walls in spots showing the slash and shapes of the wounds covering them. The shadows, weak now, came together and exploded. One shape headlocked the other. A free arm raised the knife high and the one below grabbed the hand with the knife glinting from it and coming down down down until the shape below pressed upwards so hard he thought his head was going to pop. But the weight shifted and he pressed and pressed upwards again until he found the strength to twist the hand and the blade, twist and twist until it flew away from him and landed point down in the floorboards. One shadow fell back into the darkness while the other struggled to stand.

Phyllis flickered a light on in the hallway. Slowly one shadow became human, but its character was still blurred in the softer darkness of the room. The moon had gone back into the clouds. Then the shape struggling to stand breathed hard.

Phyllis was too afraid to go all the way in. She called from the hallway, "Jordan? Are you there, Jordan?"

No answer but the pulsing room. Phyllis could smell the sweat. "Jordan, Jordan?"

The pulsing odor was stronger, louder. Phyllis held herself in and prayed. She went in and switched on the light. She gasped. Blood was everywhere. Jordan's and the man who had come into the house. The walls were spotted with it and thick pools on the floor were seeping into the wood. And there was Jordan standing, looking down, his hands red and heavy beside him, his pajama top torn open and wet. The light stung the other and he rolled his torn head to one side. He tried to speak but his lips were too swollen to move.

Jordan saw his red hands. He held his head as his fingers reached into his face and tugged feverishly. The fallen man looked up at him towering there, his face twisting madly. Through the light on the man's face Jordan saw the scar. The head rolled again. The lips tried to speak, "Jordan?" Towering there, his fingers clutching, Jordan looked away. "Jordan, son, you was mine," Jake Williams sunk back to the floor. His eyes closed deeply, his breath came slow.

"Oh, my God." Jordan looked about furiously. Phyllis stared into him speechless. "Oh my God." His fingers tugged again with fever. He hit the floor. "It's not true, it can't be true." His bleeding hands dug into the skull behind his face. He pulled at his hair. His stomach tightened with one full howl rising into his chest and filling him up so that he had to let it out and out "Aaaaaww-whhooo!" He screamed and the scream filling the red patched room, emptied him. The entire house heaved. The night was awake; the moon watched him from the window. Phyllis looked hard at him and saw what she hadn't seen before. Jordan, bleeding, mad, gone from her. And she herself was empty from all the running, from the man chasing and choking her, from the earth digging into her cut skin. She looked at him, Jordan, crawling there and whimpering. She said as coolly as if she too had nothing left inside her but the icy words to say it, "Yes it is, Jordan. It's true."

Phyllis heard the footsteps on the porch but she didn't move and neither did Jordan. They came toward the lighted room. Jeremiah was at the door. He said nothing and looked at the still man. Neither Phyllis nor Jordan spoke. Lou followed behind. The men took their cue from the silence governing the spotted floor. Jake Williams lay hard, like baked clay. They nodded and left Jake lying there.

When they had gone Jordan, crouching low, broke the silence. He spoke as much to the room as to Phyllis.

"How did you know?" he asked.

"I saw her."

"Who?"

"I saw her and I spoke to her. It was awful."

"Who?"

"Your grandmother."

"What?"

"Mother Harriet. She's alive."

At once the screaming and the bells started together inside him and filled him before he could close them out with his hands clutched to his head to keep it from splitting. *Dong Dong Dong Aaaawwwhhooo, Dong Dong Dong.* Then he sensed a rushing laughter, muffled and distant like a river rising, come toward him. The laughter reached him but he dared not look. He sank to the floor.

And there she was in his mind, Mother Harriet more alive and menacing than ever, not speeding a dream vehicle around the hairpin curve in the Mohawk hills above Ephramville, not in Jeremiah's childlike letter announcing her death and tightening its warning about his neck, but here in the cluttered room, her toothless mouth and the foul breath of her revenge: *Take the gun, Jordan. You almost a man.* He had no weapon but his fists. *Take the gun, Jordan. You a man now.* And his hands hurt. *Get him for me and for your Mama. Don't ask me that, Gran' Mama.* It was all right to eat dirt sometimes, like Mason said. But not grave dirt. Chloe's grave dirt stuck under his fingernails. *I loved Mason, Gran'Mama. I really did. "You can't love somebody until you learn about hate. You just stand there and feel it. Feel it good."* Jordan stood up. He watched his helpless father on the floor until his eyes poured out.

"She won't get away with this," he said half to Phyllis, half to the room. "I won't let her get away with this."

Jordan tore off the bedsheets and wrapped Jake in them. "Help me, Phyllis," Jordan said. They covered his wounds. Jordan lifted Jake in his arms and headed for the door. "They'll be coming back, Phyllis. We've got to get him out of here before they get back."

"Let me go with you."

"No. This is something I have to do. They'll kill him for sure this time."

"What about Mother Harriet?"

"She's waited this long, hasn't she?"

"I'm coming with you."

"I've got to do this alone."

"I'm coming with you, Jordan, and that's that."

Without another word they were gone.

THREE
The Beautiful, Beautiful River?

1

Outside it was night and chill and night and fear, a night thick with brush and footpaths, a night contending with death and despair and a night of no possible way except straight into darkness downhill between gullies and shadows of hills, and a night all alive with unthinkable insects and chirping and buzzing and a slow dripping sweat. A night full of night everywhere. It was Jordan and Phyllis and Jake. They had to get out and get going, but where? except back into night, into brush thick as hair and the night all alive with their pain. But where could they go and when would the dawn come to show them the way? Where? To the highway, to asphalt, to bridges and telephone poles? To the river and on to the road through the hills, to Rockingham out of Pee Dee on the arc of a star.

"Where are we going, Jordan?"

"We've got to get him to a hospital, Phyllis."

"There's no car!"

"If we can just make it to the highway, we'll get a ride from there."

"Think he can last?"

"We'll take the shortcut by the river and follow the dirt road down. Can you make it old man?"

Jake Williams groaned. He tried to speak. His voice was raspy, throat clogged. "Go easy with me, boy. Easy."

Jordan lifted Jake onto his back. Phyllis walked by Jordan's side, gathering up the bedsheets as they fell from Jake's shoulders. Jordan stepped cautiously, then quickly as the path became clearer in the moonlight and the warbling call of the river more distinct. Dirt loosening under foot and occasional rocks made Jordan stumble. Jake was heavy and getting heavier.

"Where you taking me?"

"You'll be all right."

"I'm hurting, son. I'm hurting real bad."

"Don't call me that," said Jordan, more to the ground ahead than to Jake's sweaty head near his own. "Don't call me son. Just hold on. We'll be there soon."

"You sure?" said Phyllis.

"It's the way I went before. When I first headed north."

They inched together down the red clay path, through brush and briars, through rock and soil.

"Jordan," said Phyllis. "He's slipping off. Hold still."

Jordan stopped and hoisted Jake further into his back. Phyllis wrapped the sheets tighter.

"Can I get me some water?" said Jake. "Water," almost mumbling.

"We'll be at the river soon."

"Can you manage?" asked Phyllis.

"He's heavy all right."

Phyllis stumbled in the darkness and reached ahead for the combined form of the men.

"But he's not as heavy as the load I've been carrying," Jordan continued.

"Are you talking about me?"

"No, Phyllis. About *me.*" *About Mason swimming towards the boat and climbing in, naked, and the sun warming the beads of riverwater dripping from his skin and his skin holding all the heat and light of a summer afternoon . . . about Jordan, suddenly afraid of deep water, holding onto him. They paddle to shore . . .* "You lucky you got a Daddy teach you how to swim," said Jordan. "I ain't that lucky," said Mason, grinning. "Yes, you is," said Jordan.

"Let's stop and rest, Jordan," said Phyllis. "You're hurt too."

"I'm all right."

"Why don't you listen to me sometimes?"

"How you doing old man? You still hurting?"

"They was gonna kill me, boy. And I comes to you and you was gonna kill me, too, huh? You my son."

"Don't call me that."

"Like Harriet and them said they'd get me. Get me if it was the last thing she do."

"You hurting, old man?"

"He's stopped bleeding, Jordan. How much farther do we have to go?"

"They was gonna kill me, and you was gonna kill me, too."

"You think you can walk some, old man. Help him down, Phyllis."

"Easy now, Jake. Lean on me. There. Jordan never thinks I can do anything."

"You think we gonna make it?" Jake said to Phyllis. Jordan watched them silently as if he were seeing the three of them more connected by design than by accident. Jake relaxed with Phyllis. And Phyllis, she was different, too.

"Let's keep out of the middle of the road," said Jordan. "In case they come looking for us."

"They might see us, huh?" said Jake.

"You walk between me and Phyllis. We won't go fast. The river isn't that far."

"River?"

"Then the highway. We'll get a ride from there."

Suddenly lights. Headlights from a pickup truck. Their three bodies gained shadows in the dust. The headlights were far off but they were coming close, coming fast. Dust spread up from the tires and made a brown halo about the searching eyes of the vehicle. The headlights glowed and swerved from side to side like a long knife cutting the night into bread.

"And we were on that road," Jordan later told Phyllis, *"Mason and I, walking home until the screeching tires from some white man's car took him away."*

"You never returned after that?"

"Never."

The river appeared out of nowhere. The surface glittered in the dark like coal. The pickup truck with its sinister eyes swerved toward them, away, and back away. It was searching. Searching.

"I loved your mama, son."

"Just Jordan, old man. Call me Jordan."

"You don't know what a pretty woman she was."

"I can tell," said Phyllis.

"But she cut me. Here on my face. Now Jordan's done cut me all up, just like they wanted him to do. They was gonna kill me."

"My baby, my baby," Mother Harriet was telling him. *"She was my baby, too,"* said Jake. *"Shit,"* she said. *"You better not come round here again."*

"Yeah, and what about the other baby?" Jake asked.

They reached the riverbank. Jordan dipped in his hand for a drink, then ducked his whole head in. Jake sipped hungrily from his own sore hands.

"Let's see about those cuts," said Phyllis, unwrapping the sheet. She tore the unbloodied parts into small bandages and washcloths. She washed where both Jordan and Jake ached. "This should hold you Jake, until we reach Rockingham."

"Hold me, hold me, baby," Jake was saying to Chloe. *"You gonna leave me?"* she asked, her voice suddenly strange to him, her hands tense.

And Mason and Jordan built a shelter out of fallen branches by the river and one night they slept in it. Arm in arm, then legs upon legs, body to body, they lay together. "Let me hold you," said Mason. "O.K." said Jordan. "Let me hold you there."

"Does it feel good?"

"Yes."

"Real good?"

"Yes. But now what happens? What're we supposed to do?"

"Pull on it. Pull on it easy, Jordan."

"Like this?"

"Yes. Yes. Oh, yesyesyesyesyes!"

"And I held him until he came, Phyllis. Like this. But that's all I did. Really. He wiped himself off with a hankey and gave the hankey to me but I didn't have anything myself then to wipe off, so I kept the hankey. I kept it like it was. Harriet said I couldn't love him like that."

"Oh, I see," said Phyllis.

"See that," said Jake pointing along the river. It was the truck again. Closer. Dust and gravel were spinning from the wheels; its headlights like roving midnight eyes. "It's them." The three crouched where they were, froze.

The pickup circled the riverbank and screeched to a halt. Voices came, then arms appeared holding guns.

"He's got to be around here somewhere."

"You see him, Jeremiah?"

"Sure, I did, Lou. Even yesterday I seen him. Don't know where they gone now. I thought Jordan had him like he should have. But they was both gone when we come back to the house, huh? Jordan gone. His wife gone. Shit."

"Mother Harriet wants him dead."

"I want him dead, too."

"Why you?"

203

"Nevermind, Lou. Just keep your eyes open."

They left the truck and searched by the water.

Jordan whispered to Jake, "Can you make it to the truck?"

"I reckon."

"Phyllis?"

"Yes."

"Then let's get the hell out of here."

They reached the open truck just in time, for Jake started coughing up blood from the quick run and his still smarting wounds. Jordan fumbled with the keys. He raced the motor. Jeremiah and Lou ran back, but suddenly stunned by highbeams aimed directly at them, they scattered apart blindly. Wheels gripped sand and gravel until the truck bounded away from the riverbank, up the grade and onto the highway.

Fifteen minutes later they were at the Rockingham General Hospital. Phyllis explained how the men were wounded in a hunting accident. Jake stayed in the hospital overnight. Jordan and Phyllis returned in the truck to Mother Harriet's house. The night was just ending. They collapsed out of fatigue in the same room where Jordan and Jake had fought.

The room still smelled of sweat and blood. Jordan was too exhausted to sleep. He sank into the room's farthest corner. What would he do now? His own confusion hemmed him in. He imagined bars of a prison rising around him. Walls stood their former distance but he was cornered in by a force which expanded and contracted in a slow pulse about him. He imagined the walls extending into space, leaving him tiny and insignificant by the room's own force against his. But the very next moment the room closed in tight, boxing him into a rat's nest. The room vibrated, pressing and pulling, stretching him in and out, demanding, urging his presence in and out. The only exit was the door he had just entered, but now it seemed to grow smaller to the tempo of invisible, pulsing flesh.

A glimmer of light shone from under the doorsill. There was still hope. Jordan decided he would come out when he was ready, when the pressing and pulling would ease long enough for him to pass through. He heard the sound of women chattering nervously beyond the opening. The chattering came louder and the corner where he lay curled was cooling off as if a source of heat and food was draining off quickly, too quickly. Then silence. Cold air. Jordan realized that the noisy chatter of women was no more than the wind playing upon the treetops.

Soon it was full morning. The room brightened. Although his eyes ached, Jordan could see Phyllis sprawled exhaustedly in the opposite corner. Her face was blank, dreamless, beyond the hold even of nightmares, real and imagined. She lay perfectly still, exuding a calm which suggested a different woman. Was she caught like Jordan and getting deeper? Was she free? The room was like a hull of skin covering him, covering them both. No, he thought. And he scratched at the skin, kicked at it, and it extended higher above him until it was invisible, gone. Once again his fear had tricked him.

Sunlight crawled under the closed door and beamed from the room's only window. Streaks of blood showed darkly on the floor and walls. Through his exhaustion and aching hands, eyes, and cramped knees, Jordan tried to think of how he got there. Someone had poked him in the night. Someone's frightened breath had covered him. The night had screamed, warning him to leave. Then a hand out of the darkness reached for him, for Phyllis. Then fists and hands and blows and glinting steel until an old man's mouth had twisted into a stutter saying, "Jordan, Jordan you was mine."

The moment the old man had spoken Jordan knew he had been alone and lonely longer than he realized. He felt diseased with incompleteness. Cast out. Somewhere inside him the broken chain of family and memory snapped shut and made him walk through the night and river and night again to safety. What did it mean? Would it be something to build upon? His face ached from the tracks left by sweat and blood. His muscles were too weak. His mouth yearned for food.

He saw Phyllis again through the mucus covering his eyes. He watched her legs, her soft thighs, her breasts heaving air as her chest expanded and contracted, pressed and pulled in steady motion. Her center had contained him, had fed him, had walked with him to the river and back. And now, he was just discovering who she was.

Her hair was tangled about her head. As the sun streaked into the room her face glowed. The sun warmed her and she stirred. The shadow of her prostrate body expanded her and she seemed to cover the entire room, covering Jordan without even moving herself. And she was warm. Jordan leaned toward her, his head protruding from what seemed like a well of flesh, a nest of dry blood, flaking old flesh, all of which had contained him. *Was it the wind again, or real women chattering and waiting and chattering?* The quiet in Phyllis's face was the same quiet of Mason sleeping soundlessly and forever under the Carolina soil. Or the quiet of his own dive into the chilly, inebriated Pee Dee at springtime. Tangles of her long loose hair were ripples from that deeply running river, were even patches of beard and hair that had covered Jake the night before, were even leaves from the trees bending away from the hill or brush cutting their clothes on a night flight from death. *He said he was his own, his son. "Don't call me that." But why, Jordan? Why? You are his son, Mother Harriet is alive.* The stillness of her body was his own immobility; her breathing, his pulsing chest, his life almost pierced by a knife. *He said I was his son.* "yesyesyesyes, yadyadyadyad" *Don't call me that,* and snapped shut the chain that had dragged so long inside him. Exhausted, Jordan crawled to Phyllis. He rested his head on her breasts and slept.

2

Mitch in bed at Aunt Clara's was thinking *somebody big, Jordan said I was somebody big* and remembering the woods and Jordan and the pines that had heard him crying. He thought of worried Maggie telling him, "just one more night. One more, until this thing with Mother Harriet settles. Then you kids can come home." He hadn't said anything about the dream. Not yet. But then the pines and Jordan made him feel he didn't have to tell her, unless of course it happens again and he can't sleep. But even then how will he say it and make the words come out right when he didn't understand all of it himself?

Ruthie had seen him coming out of the woods and wanted to know where he'd been and what had happened. She had listened there at Aunt Clara's as Mitch told her about Alfred, about Beauford teasing him again, about the hiding place she'd never find and Jordan who was there and who talked to him, gave him his jacket and said it was all right.

"You coming with me, Ruthie?"

"Where?"

"To see him next time. He says I'm gonna be somebody big."

"Who you gonna be?"

"I don't know yet, but somebody."

"Gee."

"You coming with me when I go see Jordan next time?"

"I don't know."

"You got to come, Ruthie. He my friend. It'll be fun."

"Will he like me, too?"

"Yeah. He even said so."

"You gonna tell Beauford?"

"No. We don't need him."

"Watch out, here he comes."

"Let's go to sleep. But don't forget."

"I won't."

Beauford pushed Mitch aside and climbed into bed. "You rotten little punk. Get out of here."

"I ain't done nothing."

"Running off. Getting me in trouble. Why don't you really get lost somewhere."

Somebody big, Mitch thought again. Beauford pushed him away from the bed. Mitch balled his fists up tight, jumped on him and hammered. Beauford swung at him hard and made him cry. But Mitch had hurt him too so he didn't mind the crying or Ruthie pulling him away from Beauford's swings.

"Get in bed with me," she said. "Before Aunt Clara comes and tells Mama."

"I'll get him," said Mitch through his tears. "I'll get him all right."

"You O.K.?"

"Yeah, I guess so."

"We'll go together, Mitch."

"Sure, Ruthie?"

"Yeah." She turned aside and slept. Beauford, too.

But Mitch was in the woods again and Beauford coming after him. "I'll get you, I'll get you Mitch." The wind pushing through the trees made him cold. The wind got stronger and Beauford was getting close. Trees bent and twisted in the sky. Mitch felt the rocky dirt and knew he was on the mountain again. The sky was boiling with clouds, and from where he stood he could hear the river

209

rushing below. The trees were singing and making him
cold from the wind bending and twisting them:

Yad Yad Yad Yad Yad
Pee Dee Pee Dee
Yad Yad Yad Yad Yad

Beauford was on him and grabbing. He lifted Mitch high
over the ledge. He dropped him. Mitch was falling. The
sky was dark and low. Suddenly he hit the river and went
under. When he surfaced he saw Beauford grinning from
the mountain top. Mitch tried to swim but the current was
too fast against him. He held his breath and bobbed up
and down until his skin was cold and rubbery. Around him
floated thousands of dead fish, their silver bottoms turned
up and racing with the current, racing with him, touching
him as Mitch bobbed helplessly and *yad yad yad yad yad*
fell singing from the mountain trees and sky and followed
him down down down.

He touched bottom. First soft clay, later firmer ground.
He had stopped bobbing and could stand up and wade,
but the dead fish were still with him and some had stuck
in the river soil. The odor of rotting fish filled the air.
Then Mitch saw the man towering on the shore as tall as
his father or Jordan. He recognized the jacket the man
wore, the jacket that was turned toward him, the back lean
and muscular, the face looking away. *Somebody big,* yes
somebody big, Mitch thought as he walked up to the man.
He touched the jacket he knew. When it turned to face
him, it was a grinning skeleton. The bones of one hand
held a tiny bell ringing *Ding Ding Ding.* Mitch fell back
into the muddy river soil, choking from the horror and
the smell of dead fish. The bones towering above him

clanged together like bells and the skull kept grinning at him caught with the fish and mud until blades of sunshine struck him awake. "What about that bell?" he said to himself. It was all he remembered. "Got to ask Jordan about that bell."

3

Mam'Zilie was wide awake when the bus pulled into the Trailways station in Charlotte. All she and Joetta had to do now was change for the local bus to Pee Dee. But Joetta was asleep. Mam'Zilie tried to wake her. "Come on, Joetta. *Lève-toi.*"

"Where is we, Zilie? Where we at?"

"Charlotte. We got more to go."

"My ass is already sore from all this riding, Zilie." Joetta shifted in her seat. The bus descended the highway ramp and brought the tall city buildings into view. Mam'Zilie settled back down next to her.

"I didn't sleep good neither."

"You all right?" Joetta said noticing the kerchief pulled to one side of Mam'Zilie's head, and her eyelids puffed and dark. "You look sick."

"I'm all right, I guess. *Ça va.*"

"If you ain't just tell me."

"I'm all right."

"I brought my makeup things. I brought my wigs with me. You want to put one on?"

"No, Joetta. You needs them more than me. *Pou' vrai.* All I gots to do is find Jake. *Crois-moi.* I be all right."

"Well, how I look? Is my hair on straight? You say they gots good looking men out there in Pee Dee?" Joetta straightened her blouse. "They gonna have to work for this stuff. I'm tired of getting thrown around. But why you so sad looking? We here ain't we?"

Outside the Charlotte terminal Joetta and Mam'Zilie found the local bus that ran to Rockingham and points beyond. The bus was slower than the one from New Orleans and within an hour it had stopped ten times. Joetta looked out from the window. She couldn't sleep anymore. "I'm sick of buses, Zilie. Ain't you? And I still don't know why you dragging me way out here. I don't even know where I'm at."

"*Moi non plus,*" was all Mam'Zilie said.

"I better not learn no French. Talk back at you one of these days," Joetta sulked.

Mam'Zilie could have said more, about how she needed Joetta with her and how she needed to find Jake. But she had said all that a hundred times over the past few hours trying to convince herself that Jake was near and that all she had to do was get him back. Her restless hands kept sliding her bracelets up and down, clanging them and sometimes catching her skin. Her eyes darted into the countryside. She could smell the woodsmoke and the pines. This sure ain't like the islands, she thought. No chile, this ain't like my home. "Where's that piece of paper, Joetta, what tells us where to get off? The one Jake left."

"In my hat box." Joetta pulled the hat box from the luggage rack above them and zipped it open. "Hold this," she said and sat the Afro wig in Mam'Zilie's lap. In the bottom of the box was the address Jake had scribbled among the papers he had left by the phone. "You know where that place is?" Joetta said.

"You better ask the driver."

"The driver?" Joetta sat up and looked over the backs of the seats.

"The bus driver, Joetta. Use your head."

"Give me back my wig. I'm going." Joetta put the hat box away and straightened her skirt. "Here goes nothing."

"Don't start feeling bad for yourself."

Joetta swayed down the aisle toward the driver just as

the bus was pulling into the Wadesboro station. No one
got out of the bus but people waited to get on. Mam'Zilie
could see Joetta blinking and leaning in close, her blouse
slightly opened, as the driver gave her directions. Joetta
gleamed. People squeezed past her trying to find their seats.
In a moment Joetta found hers again. "We ain't too far,"
she said climbing in next to Mam'Zilie.

"He's gonna show us. Ain't that nice of him? Ain't it?"
Mam'Zilie was quiet. "You all right, Zilie?" Ten minutes
later the bus pulled to a stop along the highway.

"All right, Miss," the driver called back. "This is your
stop. Let's go."

Mam'Zilie and Joetta looked at the desolate road and
country around them. There were pine trees and patches
of gravel everywhere, but no terminal. Not even a gas station. "Pee Dee junction," the driver said again. The women
got out.

Joetta stood near the bags that the driver had set out for
them. "Lord knows, Zilie, I sure don't know where I'm at."

"It's the Pee Dee junction," the driver said getting back
into the bus.

"But where's Pee Dee? *Où ça?*" said Mam'Zilie.

"The river's yonder. This here is Route 74. If it's the
town you want there ain't much of it left."

"We got people there," said Joetta, nudging Mam'Zilie.
"You live around here?"

"You take that road what points to Morven and Chesterfield," the driver said from his seat. "It's Highway 145.
Pee Dee around the bend there. Not far, but ain't many
folks living there now."

"Thank you Mister Driver," said Joetta. She waved her
handkerchief as the bus pulled ahead and across the Hardison Bridge and on into Rockingham.

"That road looks mighty long," said Mam'Zilie, gripping her suitcase. Her bracelets clanged as she walked. "Don't tell me we got to *walk*," said Joetta, catching up to her. The sun was beaming and sweat ran from the edges of Mam'Zilie's kerchief and Joetta's straight hair wig. "We got to find him. That's what we come for." "I know that, Zilie, but I'm already tired from all that riding." "I ain't slept neither. *Pas moin, non!*" "Look, Zilie. There's a sign." They walked to it. Joetta sat on her bags and rested while Mam'Zilie read, *Paper Company, Pulpwood Factory,* and below that in tiny letters, *Pee Dee.* The road ahead of them was deserted. Behind them the highway buzzed with activity. "Let's go, Joetta. *Allons-y.*" "I'm coming." Two cars zoomed past them and then another. Must be heading for Morven, Mam'Zilie thought. Who'd stop in Pee Dee. But where *is* Pee Dee? She looked around her and saw the empty fields. Joetta watched the road expectantly but she was already puffing and sweaty under the arms. As they moved further down the road the driver called Highway 145 the sun continued to burn. "This sure ain't like New Orleans, huh Zilie?" "No." "I sure don't know where I'm at." *"Moi non plus."* "These bags sure is heavy." "If you keep your mouth shut, Joetta, you might have some energy left. *Ferme-la.*" "So that's why you so quiet—" "I'm thinking about Jake. *C'est mon nègre, non?*" "I didn't *have* to come all the way out here, you know." "I know. But I need you Joetta. I'm sorry." Mam'Zilie stopped alongside the road and rested on her suitcase. Joetta sat next to her and wiped her face with the end of her blouse. "That's all right, Zilie. We'll find him."

A rusted yellow pickup truck came up behind them. Farming tools were piled in the back and rattled as the truck pulled to a stop. Inside Lou was smoking his pipe. "You womens needs a lift somewhere?"

Joetta tucked her blouse back in tight and straightened her wig. "Which way you going?"

"On into Pee Dee."

"Us, too. Ain't we, Zilie?" Mam'Zilie approached the truck but said nothing. "We come to see our people," Joetta said proudly.

"You got people here? What they name?"

Joetta looked at Mam'Zilie, "What they name, Zilie?"

Mam'Zilie looked at Lou. "Harriet Henry," she said slowly. She felt her stomach go light.

"Yeah, that's right," said Joetta. "Harriet Henry."

"She your people?" asked Lou. "You don't look like you from around here."

"We come from New Orleans. In Louisiana. I'm Joetta and this here's Mam'Zilie. She Jake Williams's wife. You married?"

Lou studied the woman beside Joetta. "Jake Williams?"

"We looking for him," Mam'Zilie said, her voice still slow.

"Well, you don't have to look far."

"This is Pee Dee, ain't it?" said Joetta, nudging Mam'Zilie. "The place ain't far is it?"

Lou looked puzzled.

"She mean the house. Where Harriet Henry stay. The house." Mam'Zilie said, almost touching the truck.

"No, mam," said Lou. "I don't reckon he's there."

Joetta stuck her face up angrily, her hands on her hips.

"You mean we come all the way from New Orleans and that nigger ain't here!"

Mam'Zilie shot her a glance.

"I'm sorry, Zilie, but I'm tired. Shit. He ain't even here."

"It ain't like Jake," said Mam'Zilie. "It just ain't like him."

Lou watched the women carefully. "I don't know where he is now. But I know where he was. They cut him up real bad last night."

"*Non! Bon Dieu, non,*" cried Mam'Zilie. A bag dropped out of her hands and popped open on the road spilling out kerchiefs, powders, assorted bottles that broke and stained the tar. Mam'Zilie held onto the truck, trying not to fall. But her eyes rolled quickly to the back of her head.

"It ain't true," said Joetta. "It can't be true, Zilie," she said as the other woman collapsed in her arms.

"I seen him myself," said Lou. He got out of the truck. "Let me help you with her," he said to Joetta, her mouth open and breathless. "Put her in the truck. You too. The place ain't far."

The pickup shifted gears and lurched forward. Mam'Zilie recovered just as they were leaving the highway and entering a winding road. Mam'Zilie studied the road and the streaks of orange above marking the afternoon sun. A sign, she thought. She needed a sign to tell her what to do. Then she saw the river and the red-orange reflection of sun. River, she thought. *The sun and the river. The house, the hill, the river. The head turning in the water, the sun turning back.* Then she knew.

"I seen it," she said aloud. "I seen that river."

"What are you talking about?" said Joetta.

"That's the Pee Dee," said Lou. He drove ahead into the sunset cutting the hills and trees into night.

217

"Just like I thought, *moin!*" said Mam'Zilie. "*Ç'est ca.*"
And she started singing alone this time:

Tumba Walla, Bumba Walla
Jake-a Walla, Jake-a
Tumba Walla, Bumba Walla
Jake-a Walla, Jake-a

4

Later that morning Jordan and Phyllis had returned in Jeremiah's truck for Jake in the hospital. It was past six o'clock by the time they could head back to Pee Dee. Jake sat quietly until broken vials of varicolored glass and kerchiefs like fallen kites appeared on the road. He made Jordan stop the truck. "It's Zilie," he said. "She's followed me here."

"Who's Zilie?" asked Phyllis.

"Zilie is Mam'Zilie. My woman. You think they gonna get her too?"

"No," said Jordan. "They wanted you Jake. We'll settle all that."

"What about Zilie?"

"We'll find her. First we've got to see Mother Harriet while she can still talk."

"Like she talked to me," said Phyllis. "Then you'll believe it."

"I believe it already, Phyllis."

"Do I have to see her?" said Jake.

"Yes," said Jordan. "It wouldn't be complete without you."

"You sound like you know something, boy."

"It took me long enough."

When they reached the house by the dirt road the sun had stretched west into afternoon. Jeremiah was sitting in the porch rocking chair. As soon as the truck drew near, Jeremiah got up and went for his gun. Jordan got out of the truck and walked straight up to him. "That was you last night, wasn't it?"

"I don't know what you talking about, Jordan," he said turning quickly from him and eyeing Phyllis and Jake moving from the truck and onto the porch.

"We'll find out soon enough," said Jordan. He motioned for the others to follow him in. Jake held onto Phyllis's extended arm, his eyes wide, betraying apprehension of Jeremiah and of what he expected from Mother Harriet inside.

"She's been waiting for you a long time," said Jeremiah. "You too, Jake. A real long time."

Jordan reached in his pockets and with a sarcastic sweep of his hand handed the truck keys to Jeremiah.

"Now ain't that something," said Phyllis.

Jeremiah said nothing.

Jordan entered the house first and motioned Jake to remain in the front room until needed. Jeremiah stood by with the gun. Jordan took a diver's breath and entered the bedroom. Phyllis followed behind. There lay Mother Harriet propped up with three pillows. Maggie was clearing away food. Mother Harriet's eyes found Jordan's and he stopped in his tracks. She still commanded attention. For a split second, he obeyed.

Jordan stood like a soldier and Mother Harriet studied him. To Jordan she could command life and death over him with the same easy effort she used to command it over herself. Jordan was certain that even if she had died long ago her spirit would have lingered eternally between the river and the house at the top of the hill, moving its tedious way into the lives of her family, those living and those dead. She had an unnameable power to burn into him: Jordan, the sole inheritor, the guardian, when she was gone, of her future in the other world; Jordan the connection between her departed spirit and the voice of the living. He was hers from the time he had entered the world on the night carriage of his mother's screams lifting him out and up from the bleeding floor to her, Mother Harriet. But he had wronged her. He left the earth that had fed him.

Jordan waited. His eyes sank deeper into his skull. His head grew heavy, his hair felt like prickly pine needles, and he would not speak until he knew he could make sense, that whatever he said might ease the pain of his return and the steady suffering in Mother Harriet's slow death. But he also wanted to speak for everything that he had learned and for the man whose life he had saved with his own.

"M-M-M-Mother Harriet," his first words stuttered out. The falling inside him stopped. He had reached the bottom of the well. Blood rushed to his feet and settled there as he stood as solitary and as insignificant as a grain of sand. The water filling Mother Harriet's face threatened to overflow. The voice of the rising river sounded in his head. The hissing breakwater at the ocean's mouth was pulling him in deep, swallowing him. But he was fighting, now, and he knew where to hit.

"You. You left *me*." Mother Harriet's words hammered at him. The well filling up. Her words reverberated from the stone hard walls about him. "You left."

"Yes."

"You left."

"But I'm here now. I've come back."

"Why, Jordan?"

"You told me. Remember? You told me about the star, Mother Harriet. The North Star. You showed me where it was and I followed it."

"You left me."

"It wasn't you I was leaving."

"And you come back?"

"Yes."

"Why?"

"I thought you were—"

"Yes?"

Silence interrupted him. Words caught in his throat.

"I er—"

"Say it, son."

"I thought you were dead."

"I am dead."

"No, you're not."

"I died when you left me."

"But a man came to the house. A man—"

"You used to call me Gran'Mama."

"Yes, Gran'Mama. But the man—"

"I knows son."

"He came into the house. I thought you were dead."

"He your daddy, Jake. Jake Williams."

"But—"

"He killed your Mama."

"How?"

"Leaving her. And just when she needed him the most. He left her just as sure as you were born. Chloe grieved after that man so long that she died. Now I got to die, but I wants to die with a clean heart."

"You want me to say I did it. I killed him?"

"Yes."

"But why, Gran'Mama. Why all this? I don't understand it."

"No?"

"You can tell me."

"You is the gift, son."

"What?"

"The gift. You is the gift cause you done come back to save me. Me and Chloe. Save yourself, too."

"But Gran'Mama, Mother Harriet, how can I—"

222

"You done come back. I can die now with a clean heart, can't I? I done lived too long. The river of my days done dried up all around me. Nothing left but mud. Now you back, I got my peace. You done saved me. Know me, chile. Remember me. It ain't too late."

"How can I—"

"Call my name in the nights. I'll hear you."

"But me, Gran'Mama. How have I saved you?"

She mumbled indistinctly. Pain inched fast from her stomach and tightened her chest. "You done come back. You killed him and we free. We free. You hear me, Chloe? He come back, Chloe."

Jordan looked at Phyllis and moved closer to the bed. Phyllis followed. Mother Harriet's eyes widened with near pleasure. The pain subsided, escaping her momentarily, just long enough for her voice to raise clear and loud like the last long wail of a siren, or the last scraping brush of a falling tree. "Touch me," she said. "Please touch me." Phyllis reached. Jordan stopped her.

"No," said Jordan.

"Please."

"No, Gran'Mama."

"Please."

"You don't really love me. How can you love me when you never loved him? How can you?"

"But I can die with a clean heart now, son."

"Don't you want to forgive me? Don't you want to forgive *him,* Gran'Mama."

"You made me rest easy, son."

"Is that all you want?"

"I'm dying with a clean heart, son."

"No, you're not, Gran'Mama."

"You made me rest easy, boy. You did. You come back.

223

You killed him and we free, now touch me, let me feel you close, so I'll know I'll be remembered."

"No, Gran'Mama. I can't do that."

Phyllis took Jordan's hand in hers. "Jordan," she said. "I'm here, too."

"We can't," he said to Mother Harriet.

Mother Harriet sat up with a start, her eyes peering into Jordan, trying to hold him with weakening effect.

"You really don't want me," said Jordan. "You want revenge. I know that at least, now."

"Jordan, touch me."

"But I won't let you have it."

Mother Harriet looked at Phyllis, her eyes pleading now for a place in their memory, a place in which she would live forever, be remembered by name and deed. "You, you his wife. Touch me, please."

"Don't move, Phyllis."

"But Jordan, she's dying."

"Don't move." Jordan looked at Harriet. "You said I was the gift come back, didn't you? Isn't that enough, Gran' Mama? Isn't it?"

Mother Harriet nodded yes then no, her head moving with increasing pain.

"Then you don't need Jake dead, do you? Do you?"

Her head stiffened. "Yes, I do, boy. For Chloe."

"Chloe's gone."

"Touch me."

"You've got no family left, Gran'Mama."

"Touch me, Jordan. Don't let me slip away."

"No. Not until you forgive him."

"No."

"Not until you forgive Jake and me."

"Jordan please touch me."

224

"You have to forgive him," Jordan turned away from the bed and headed for the door.

"Please, Jordan."

"Come in, Jake," Jordan said to the open doorway. And Jake walked in silently, his head almost bowed. Then he looked straight at Mother Harriet. "Forgive him, Gran'Mama."

Jake said nothing.

"Chloe, Chloe my pretty baby . . ."

"You have to save yourself, Gran'Mama. You still have a chance."

"Touch me."

"Forgive him."

"Forgive me," said Jake, his voice clear and direct, his eyes fast on Harriet's.

"I'm dying, son. Don't let me slip away."

"Help yourself, Gran'Mama. And help us."

"Yes," she said weakly.

"Forgive him," said Jordan. "Forgive Jake."

"I loved Chloe," said Jake. "And this is my boy."

"I'm his wife," said Phyllis. "Help us."

"Yes," said Mother Harriet. "Yes, yes, yes. You all mine. Touch me."

And they held onto Mother Harriet tight. Phyllis's hands circled the woman's leathery stomach, Jordan held her hands, and Jake touched her wrinkled feet. Mother Harriet grabbed Phyllis's hand and led it from her stomach to her belly and to the dry hollow between her legs. Heat from the dying flesh crawled into Phyllis and into Jordan and into Jake.

"Yes," said Mother Harriet, almost crooning. "Yes, yes," softly, then loud, "yesyesyesyesyes" until the word was a musical note between them, a note of song and ease and relief, a note against pain, sealing her bond with them forever,

> *"yesyesyesyesyes*
> *yadyadyadyadyad."*

And the melody carried itself out the window and up through the air and on through the tops of the pines rustling now with the wide presence of her voice. The vessel of body which had locked those words for years found relief and rest.

Phyllis's hand at the hollow cooled but she did not move, she couldn't move. Something held it there until the skin grew cold. She looked at Jordan, at Jake, and at the head cuddled under Jordan's hand. A glint of hope had frozen into Mother Harriet's open brown eyes staring ahead. Her lips slanted into a smile. Jordan closed her marble eyes.

Maggie and Jeremiah, gathered at the door, moved further into the room. Maggie pushed back the patchwork quilts and the soiled linen and offered to the setting sun Mother Harriet's bent body. Jordan, after a moment's hesitation, kissed the hard bony forehead. No one cried. Jake stood quiet and still. Jordan was as dry as an autumn leaf. Jeremiah motioned them all outside.

Jordan moved to sit down in the front room but Jeremiah stopped him with his fists. "You god-damn black-assed bastard!" His face went livid. His body was ready to explode. "You let her die, nigger," he cried, pulling Jordan into his chest that was knotted with grief. His hands were shaking, his eyes red. He had Jordan by the shirt and wouldn't let him go.

Maggie pushed between them. "Stop it, Jeremiah. Stop it. Stop it, I say."

226

Jake stepped in, "You let go my boy. He ain't nothing to you."

Jordan pulled away as Jake and Maggie hustled Jeremiah into an empty chair and held him there. He sat sulking. Jordan remained silent and calm until Jeremiah's eyes found him.

"What's bothering you, Jeremiah?" asked Jordan.

Jake spoke up. "You ain't got nothin' to say."

But Jordan was weary, a man almost defeated by all sides. Hadn't Mother Harriet vindicated him in her last words? Hadn't his return solved all of it for her? Didn't the family snap itself back together? She had called him the gift. Gift? Jordan looked to the others for an answer. Phyllis sat with her hands cupped in her lap, the fingers moving silently. Jake's glazed stare suggested calm. Jeremiah was boiling in his chair. Maggie rested her head on his knees.

"It was me," Jeremiah said. "Me who took care of her all these years. She was mine too. My own and Maggie's. But you, you sullen professional punk of a colored boy, who you think been giving that woman some hope and life for the last twenty years? Who you think been telling her yes there's something else to live for, and yes, there's something else to love besides an ugly black bastard off somewheres hiding, or a drunk soaking in his own puke. We done what you was too proud and too busy to do. We gave her what you didn't have. Love. You understand that? Shit, Mister Pro-fessor. Yeah, you left her and didn't give one good goddamn. She deserved her peace."

Jake stood up. "My boy done what he could," he said. "You got two of us to tangle with now, you keep messing, hear."

"But we found her," Maggie said to her husband, her hands soothing his knees, then reaching for his chest. "And we loved her just the same."

"I wants to know why, Jordan," Jeremiah said.

"She knows," he answered. "Mother Harriet knows."

"You tell *me* why."

Jake leaned over Jeremiah. "He ain't got to tell you nothing. I'm the one to tell it, ain't I?"

"I don't owe you a thing, Jeremiah," said Jordan, getting up, too, and closer to Jeremiah. "Mother Harriet is free now. That's all that matters. You leave me alone." Jordan looked at Jake, then Phyllis. "You leave *us* alone."

"Got two of us to tangle with now, you hear."

Jeremiah looked up, his eyes watery and hard. "So you all can get rich off the land, huh?"

"Your blood's here too, Jeremiah," said Jordan. "I can't deny you that."

"And yours!" said Jeremiah. "You better find some life in it, boy. Some life." His lips trembled as he spoke and kept on trembling as though he could leap at Jordan any minute and cut him too for the blood he needed to feed his commitment. But he sank deeper into the chair and held his greying head in his hands. Maggie comforted him as he sobbed, his mouth pursed in anger and grief. His eyes blinked fast to stem the tears that were quickly filling his face and tying more knots inside him. Maggie's face was wet and wrinkled, too.

"I have," said Jordan. "I've found some life here."

"Me, too," said Jake. "And you ain't got nothing to do with it, Mister Jeremiah Willis."

Phyllis took Jordan and Jake by the hand. "Let's go. I can't stand any more fighting."

"Wait a minute," said Maggie, she turned to Jeremiah still silent in his chair. "I'm sorry, Jeremiah, but maybe they're right about something. She had us trapped. Mother Harriet had us trapped, honey."

"My God," said Jeremiah. "My God."

"And now you want to trap us," said Jordan.

Jeremiah said nothing. Jake grinned.

"Look at me, Jeremiah," said Jordan uneasily, "You know I'm not fooling you. I can't go back to what I was as a child, or even who I was up north before coming back here. Not now. Not after all this." Jordan looked straight at Jake, then to Phyllis and back to Jeremiah. "And I think you already know that. Listen, I saw Mitch, your youngest boy. We talked together, and we'll talk together again. Your blood's here, too, Jeremiah. Stronger than mine. I'm here yes, but I'm not tied here. Trapped? I don't know. This is my home, Jeremiah. Our home. You're family, too. I can't sell the land away like that. I just can't do it. If that's what you're afraid of, you can stop worrying. But you can't keep me here because of that."

Just then a truck halted in the driveway. Voices, excited voices came into the house riding on a gust of red dust and rock.

"You shore this the house, Mister Lou?"

"Go on in."

"Zilie, my feets hurt. I can't be going house to house."

"Hush, Joetta."

When Jake heard them he rushed out from the front room. "Zilie, Zilie!"

"Jake!"

"Hot diggity, Zilie. It's you."

"Oui, mon nègre. Que Dieu est bon!"

"What's all that talk?" said Maggie.

"Languages," said Jeremiah.

Joetta burst into the tiny front room with Lou and Mam'Zilie and Jake trailing behind. "We from New Orleans," Joetta said. "We family."

229

No one said a word.

"We come all the way by bus," Joetta continued, her eyes wide about the room and the speechless people.

Mam'Zilie motioned for quiet. "Hush, Joetta. There's death about in this house. *Baron Samedi est là. Li-là.*"

"Who dead?" Joetta asked around. "Tired seem like it to me."

"Mother Harriet," said Jake.

"And who's he?" said Joetta, pointing.

"That's Jordan. He my son."

"He do have a son, Mam'Zilie." Joetta came closer to Jordan. "You married?"

"This is Phyllis, my wife."

And Phyllis said, "Yes. I'm his wife."

"Well, I'm Joetta. From New Orleans. This here's Mam'Zilie. She my friend. Jake my friend, too." She turned to Jake, her voice softer now, relaxed as smoke curling into the air. "I knew you wasn't a mean man, Jake."

Mam'Zilie chuckled uneasily, eyeing the crowd. "*Mon nègre.*"

"And you his wife?" said Joetta looking at Phyllis.

"I'm Phyllis."

"You all from around here? We from Louisiana. New Orleans. Huh, Jake?"

"Yeah."

"I was born here," said Jordan.

"You Harriet's boy?"

"No, grandson. My mother died when I was born."

"Chloe," said Mam'Zilie. She moved closer to Jake and held him. "It was Chloe, weren't it? *Je le sais, moin. Connais bien.* You used to call her name out in your sleep. I never said nothing. *Rien, pas moin.* But it made me feel funny just to hear you calling like that in your sleep. *Pas comprend, moin.*"

230

"I ain't a mean man," said Jake. He turned to Jeremiah and silent Maggie. "I ain't a mean man. And neither is my boy here."

"We was all trapped," said Maggie. "Ain't it the truth, Jeremiah? Ain't it?"

Jeremiah said nothing, and he didn't move.

"Scared of her, weren't you Jake?" said Mam'Zilie. "She dead now. Sometimes you was so far from me, Jake. And I was scared I couldn't get you back."

Jake hugged Mam'Zilie tighter.

"And he almost killed him," said Lou. "Yeah, Jordan almost killed him."

"I almost killed a man," said Jordan, more to himself than to anyone else.

"Mother Harriet's gone now," said Phyllis, putting her hand in Jordan's hand.

"I used to live in that house," Jordan said.

"She was Mother Harriet to us all," said Jeremiah. "All of us."

"And your kids, Jeremiah? What are you going to tell them about it, about me, about yourself? What about Mitch and Ruthie and the oldest one. You just did Mother Harriet's bidding, right? And all she really wanted was to see Jake dead."

"And you come back," said Jeremiah. "She wanted you back. I wanted you back."

"But why, Jeremiah? Why?"

He said nothing. He didn't move.

"She was his grandmother," said Phyllis to Joetta. "I saw her with my own eyes. I touched her, too."

"He ain't a mean man," said Joetta. "We sang a song about you, Jake. We wanted you back. Ain't that right, Zilie? You got your man now."

"*Oui, c'est mon nègre.*"

231

"Now all I got to do is find me one." And Joetta started humming the song they sang before and Mam'Zilie joined her in humming, her bracelets clanging against her skirt like bells.

"You all must be tired," said Phyllis. "There's room up on the hill. Harriet's house."

"Yes," said Jordan. "Follow me."

And all left except Jeremiah and Maggie, silent in the doorway.

5

Later that evening Addie Miller went walking. Her cane tapped the ground to make sure it was steady enough to hold her. This time it wasn't the hill leading to Harriet Henry's house that she had to climb, and her friend was no longer rocking there to greet her. This road was straight. From the house ahead lights shone from the room where Mother Harriet's body lay. Someone was rocking on the front porch, peacefully, just like Harriet herself, as silent and as old as the earth, rocking and waiting. Addie came nearer and saw that it was Jeremiah. "Evening," she said.

Jeremiah said nothing. He stopped rocking.

"She was my friend, too, Jeremiah. You know that."

"Maggie waiting on you. Funeral tomorrow."

"Preacher Franklin know already, huh?"

"Yeah."

"I was eating my dinner when Lou come tell me," Addie said, leaning towards the window and the back screen door. Maggie was inside getting things ready to clean the body. "But I'm glad Jeremiah. I ain't crying cause I'm glad. She suffered too long. Too long."

"Yeah."

"She was my friend and I'm glad she resting."

"Maggie waiting on you, Addie."

In a moment Addie was gone behind the screen door, gone to get hot water and soap and Sunday clothes. Tomorrow was going to be Harriet's special day.

Jeremiah stayed on the porch to watch the night come into the woods. He heard birds, then a truck rumble from far off. When it screeched around the bend and jumped into gear for the hill, he knew it was Lou. Jeremiah stood up and watched the red dust rise from the road behind the pickup. Then he left the porch and the chair rocking empty. He took the path behind the house and climbed the hill. When he reached Mother Harriet's backyard, the truck had just parked. Lou and Joetta climbed out of the cabin with packages of groceries. They were laughing. Joetta's mouth was wide. Lou pinched her on the behind as they entered through the back door. Jeremiah came forward, unseen. He surveyed the house and the red clay drive, the overlook from the hill. "This is mine," he said aloud to no one but himself, "All mine. And Jordan ain't got shit to do with it."

And the ground answered as if everything buried there or lingering in the breeze before burial had voice saying, "Yes you have it. Yes it is yours,

yesyesyesyesyesyesyes
yadyadyadyadyadyadyad

Yad. Yad." And Jeremiah turned away from the house and the red clay hill and followed the voice back through the wide deserted cornfield.

6

The next afternoon Jordan found himself before a grave. His feet anchored in the mound of fresh clay beneath him. Phyllis came to his side and slipped her hand in his.

Someone was reading, "I am the resurrection and the life." But Jordan had heard it all before, years ago, when a little black boy slept alone in the North Carolina ground: red, like the color of dried blood; hard, like the stiff trunks of pines. The face inside the coffin could not hear the words, so why say them, Jordan thought. But were they for him, those words spoken into the ground like that? No, Jordan was sure. Not for him. There were no words left to be spoken, or read, or heard. He wanted to dissolve the preacher's slow voice and its artificial dignity. The words sounded as empty as Jordan although he was standing there and watching the mound pile high and counting the clumps of clay at his feet. He tried to focus on the smaller grains and pebbles, but he could not think. Someone inside him echoed the official voice from far away, *I am the resurrection and the life.*

The blackness of the hole was beautiful and deep. Jordan wanted to lie inside, caress the hard clay sides and feel the earth drop loosely through his fingers as it fell upon him, straight and cold, and until it shut out all the sunlight and burning within. Worms would be his new friends, eating his eyes out first so he could no longer see the old woman's face pasted on his brain. He would be anonymous, invisible and free. He wanted her to forget him just as he tried to forget her and himself for years.

With a soft thud Rev. Franklin committed Mother Har-

235

riet to the earth. Jordan listened for the soil dropping onto the coffin and spilling from the sides, filling up. He heard the voice again. Was time standing still? *I am the . . .* What was he? The heaving in his chest tried to answer.

Maggie held Phyllis's hand and Jeremiah's arm found Jordan's shoulder. A delegation of elders from the Good Shepherd filed to the grave. Two men planted a wreath at the head. Ladies behind them started to sing,

> In the cross, in the cross
> Be my glory ever.
> Till my raptured soul shall find
> Rest beyond the river.

The words iced into Jordan, who watched as the grave settled.

From the group came Addie Miller, hobbling with her cane. She stopped in front of Jordan and looked hard. Her eyes brightened. She smiled wide, showing few remaining teeth. Her mouth moved faster than the words she spoke, "Boy, I knows you. I know I knows you. Remember me? Addie, Addie Miller?" Jordan nodded. "I'm sure glad to see you," she said. "Yes I am. You come back. Well, God bless you. Didn't Harriet look good?"

Jordan nodded.

"She sure looked good. And I'm glad to see you, Jordan. Welcome home. Welcome." Addie kissed him and hobbled up to the fresh grave. "You sure looked good, Harriet. Real good."

Later, from the porch, Jordan and Phyllis watched the sun set and the night crawl over the mountains and roads. Purple hazes rose fully into the sky as blue faded to grey, then to the soft blackness which is the beginning of night.

236

Below the porch Jordan heard a car pull into Jeremiah's yard. He could hear the laughter and excitement of children returning home. He felt alive. There was life down there. He wanted a piece of it, but in his own way. Maybe he could find the words to tell Mitch about it. Or a freshman back at Ephram College. *Mitch,* he thought again and breathed deeply. Phyllis was silent next to him. He could feel her warmth. The air around him stirred with a river breeze that calmed him, telling him that it was his if he wanted it, all of it, the land, the river, and the night. He could take it.

Phyllis pulled Jordan in from the porch. "Let's sleep now," she said softly, conspiratorially.

"I almost killed a man, honey. And goddammit, that man is my father."

"It's over now. Mother Harriet's dead."

"I sure hope it's over."

"Come sleep now."

On their way to the back bedroom, Jordan stopped at Mother Harriet's living room where Jake and Mam'Zilie were dipping snuff by the fireplace. "You knew Jake was alive, didn't you, Mam'Zilie?" Jordan asked.

"I know everything about Jake, *mon cher.* I was scared you didn't."

"Me, too," said Jake. "I was scared, too."

"You'll go back to New Orleans?" asked Phyllis.

"It's better that way, *non?*"

"Yeah, we really don't belong here, do we, Zilie?"

"Now you know, Jake."

"But Mam'Zilie," said Jordan.

"Yes?"

"You knew all about it all along, didn't you?"

"*Non,* not all of it. *Pas moin.* Then again I don't give all my secrets out. You'll find a way for yourself, Jordan.

You too, Phyllis. I'm happy for you. And I'm happy for us."

"I know my way now," said Jordan.

Jake rose from his seat and hugged Jordan, then Phyllis.

"Thank you, son. Am I gonna see you again?"

"I don't know. I'm glad just knowing you're there."

"Me, too, son. And daughter. How you like that, Zilie, got me a daughter, too."

"*C'est bon.*"

"Tomorrow, Zilie, we getting the hell out of here."

"Goodnight, children. *Bonne nuit le'zenfants.*"

"Goodnight."

Then laughter and smooth voices came from the next room behind the living room, Mother Harriet's spare room. Mam'Zilie hushed the gathering so they could listen. Joetta's voice came full of breath, irregular and deep. "You ever been there?" she was saying. Lou grunted, moaned. "You ever been right at the mouth of the Mississippi?"

Hands to their faces, Jake and Mam'Zilie suppressed their laughs and waved goodnight. Phyllis led Jordan away to the bedroom.

Once there she went to the suitcase and got the pink paper she had written on and set it beside the bed. Jordan took his clothes off slowly. He felt sleepy and comfortable. Phyllis waited for him in bed. She reached for his waist and pulled him tight. Their lips gave open full kisses suggesting hunger and food. Phyllis held him tighter and wrenched him deep in her thighs. "Forever," she whispered in his ear, "forever." She felt the lines of his skin etch into hers, *home is the earth of you.*

They rolled naked together across the bed and back again, knocking the broken blue fishing pole and the unlatched metal box to the floor with a sharp clang. The noise escaped both of them and drowned in their sweating hips as Phyllis released herself to him. *The treasure,* she thought, *of you I am.* Jordan sank deeper into her. She was as moist and surging as the river itself and Jordan swam inside her, mixing his stream into her tide. *The earth of you I am,* she felt herself heave and the heat fill her. "I feel it Jordan," she whispered. "The heat." And they swam in the warm sweat covering them, protecting them from pain. Sleep would not win them tonight. Phyllis felt her belly growl and throb. It was absorbing all the wetness around and in her. She knew then that a treasure had been within her all the while. Jordan's gentle probing this time had released it from her and into him and back again in the common surge and swell of rivers.

7

Meanwhile, below the house, instead of going straight to bed as Maggie had told them, Mitch and Ruthie stole out of the back window when Beauford had fallen asleep. They ran up the hill and found a spot on Harriet Henry's back porch. Ruthie was already out of breath. Mitch tried to calm her as he looked up to see if anyone had seen them.

"But Mitch, we supposed to be sleep."

"I know. But we can wait here."

"What's Mama gonna say when she gets up and we ain't there. Suppose Beauford tells on us?"

"He didn't see us. He was asleep. Did you take the blanket?"

"Yeah. But I almost dropped it running."

"We can sleep here on the porch. It ain't too cold."

"You sure Jordan said we can come here?"

"Yeah, I'm sure Ruthie. He told me himself."

They snuggled together against the outer wall just under the kitchen window so that Jordan wouldn't hear them. The night was singing around them, but it was warm and the mosquitoes left them alone. Mitch slept soundly without dreams, leaning against his sister and the wood plank house.

And dawn caught Phyllis and Jordan awake. She rolled to his side and put his hand on her lower stomach. Jordan felt the place where heat throbbed and radiated through her body. Phyllis kissed his sweating hollow cheeks that seemed to burn with the same something she felt was planted inside her.

Phyllis watched as the room brightened into morning. She got up and went to the window. She saw the rich black land stretch for miles ahead of her. She felt it was a part of her now. She saw the cornfields and the pine forest naked and waiting. She listened for its voice. She was reminded just for an instant of the hymn Jordan sang and the lines scribbled on the loose page. She felt words moving in her mind to something she had to write down quickly before it faded. She found the pink page beside the bed and wrote. "There," she said aloud. "Finished."

"Come back to bed Phyllis."

"I have it now, Jordan. The poem. Listen, but don't laugh."

"I promise," Jordan sat up.

Phyllis held the page nervously and read:

> *I am the earth: black, red, brown*
> *I feel your tree, the home is here.*
> *You corner seeds and scratch the sky*
> *Nest a bird and make him fly.*
> *Tree, how still and strong to me*
> *Your root of pain and misery,*
> *As the earth of you I am, will be.*

"There," said Phyllis and moved closer to Jordan who was smiling and reaching for her. But then she heard something like a human voice growling or laughing. Jordan heard it too. His skin cooled. His smile vanished. Phyllis turned sharply to the window. It was the sound they both remembered from dying Mother Harriet, who seemed to be calling from the woods beyond the window. Phyllis

241

snuggled close to Jordan. The sound became more distinct. It wasn't laughter, but a song, and the sun came so bright it burned through the window.

"It's never over is it?" said Phyllis.

"Never. We have to go back, Phyllis."

"You mean north, right?"

"Yes, even if it's just to leave again."

"It's never over."

"We're always beginning again.

Outside the house Ruthie was awake first. She nudged Mitch. "You up yet?"

"Yeah."

"What's that noise? I thought we was going to see Jordan."

"Sounds like a woman, a crazy woman singing."

"Sounds like Beauford."

"I'm scared, Mitch."

"Me, too."

"You think he's in there? Your friend Jordan."

"He told me to come back."

"You sure?"

"Yeah, I'm sure."

"But what about that noise, it's scary."

"Let's ask him."

They went in.

The laughing song in the air woke Maggie and she tried to wake Jeremiah but he rolled back to sleep. Maggie felt uneasy and went to check on the children. She saw Beauford, then the empty bed. Maggie shook him awake.

"Beauford, Beauford!"

"Aw, Mama."

"Where's Mitch? Where's Ruthie?" Maggie shook him again. "Beauford!"

The coarse singing fell from the hill,

yes yes yes yes yes
yad yad yad yad yad

and it drilled into her as Beauford, smiling, searched the bed for empty spaces.